T0109020

GATHER THE FACES

GATHER THE FACES

BERYL GILROY

PEEPAL TREE

First published in Great Britain in 1996
Peepal Tree Press Ltd
17 King's Avenue
Leeds LS6 1QS

Second printing 2001

© Beryl Gilroy 1996

All rights reserved
No part of this publication may be
reproduced or transmitted in any form
without permission

ISBN 0 948833 88 2

Gather the faces if you wish it so,
Gather the faces and keep them.

In loving memory
P.E. Gilroy
1919-1975

CHAPTER ONE

A postcard arrived from my two middle-aged aunts! How that card takes me back to the moment they came into my life. They are now in Barbados and widowed again. Fate had not allowed them time to be mothers. As young women they had married two brothers, both fishermen. They were lost to the fury of those winds that wandered from the ocean to the rivers to overwhelm small craft. When they were widowed the first time, they occupied themselves by looking after my mother, the youngest of the sisters, until she married, and their two parents, until the latter both passed away. Support, comfort, and sustenance came from the Church of the Holy Spirit, an offshoot of the Black Protestant communion. My aunts lived by a hierarchy of necessities. It was necessary for this or that or the other to happen. My aunts became surrogate mothers to the needy, friends to the crushed and the downtrodden, whether men, women or children. Mother, as a girl, was fiercely protected. That was necessary. Like her sisters, her dark-brown body had been sculpted into a straight-limbed, long-legged creation. Her features were skilfully and deftly marked, her flowing tresses fell to her shoulders. And then, as if to render her more enigmatic, the dainty frill of her mouth smiled at the most unexpected moments. Her looks were a temptation to wicked men.

When she was eighteen, mother married. Another necessity. Her husband, my father, Samson Payne, had been, like her, raised in the Anglican Church. But his position as a semi-indentured plantation carpenter meant that he had to travel a lot. On the estate, they were only given seasonal work — not enough to survive on. But moving from one village to another had its advantages. It placed him beyond the tentacles of the Anglican Church bigots, and his desire to better himself caused him to review the achievements of the Church of the Holy Spirit, and join them.

My mother and father fought with life and survived. When mother became pregnant, life grew harder. How did she get pregnant? She wept in the darkness and prayed regularly for God's guidance. It should have been a moment of rejoicing but they clung to each other in despair. Another life to join the shirt-tail boys and girls outside. Other harsh realities. Other cries of need. Mother took in sewing.

'No,' said my father. 'This will never do. I am a competent carpenter.' He wrote letters and to cut a long story short, he left mother to the mercy of the Church of the Holy Spirit and her sisters, and took the boat to England. He had been recruited to work for British Railways.

I was three when we joined him in St. Pancras. We occupied a little flat in Goldington Crescent, not far from the railway yard where he now worked. My mother was a skilled stitcher. She stitched dresses from home — piecework they called it.

I went to school and came home to play hide and seek with myself, hiding behind the piles of clothes, a repressed child, obedient, willing to please, able to express my feelings only in the security of our own home. Hungry for tenderness. Shy and hesitant. My mother had no time for conversation. Everyone gave orders.

My father worked all hours, even at weekends, and eventually saved enough to buy a little mid-terrace house in the next street. It was not a beautiful place, quite unlike the greenness we had left behind. At the back of the house, a bombed out block stared at us, like a gaping mouth full of broken teeth. It represented what I had been taught of the world, the flesh and the devil.

No one had told me about the imminent arrival of my aunts. One day, in the dusk of early autumn, I opened the door and there they were. They hugged me and held me. I did not respond with the eagerness of familiarity. I stared beyond them into the sky, with its smudges of orange and crimson. I looked up at the designs made by birds flying overhead.

'Kiss me!' ordered a voice, and I plonked a sticky kiss on my aunt's face. She tasted sweet. I remembered her then. She was Mavis, the aunt who, I was to discover, put honey and lime juice on her skin. I kissed Julie.

'Marvina', they said to my mum, 'What a nice child you have here, man. The child can kiss. Where she learn that from? Mouth open like that?'

My aunts had come to live with us. They took me over and changed my school to a Church school. It reminded me of a respectable old woman dressed in threadbare dresses and tattered lace petticoats. The children were nicer and my godsister, Sherri, two years older than I was, had gone there.

Later, I became a competent typist, left school at sixteen and got a job typing for London Transport. I learned shorthand. I was well set up for secretarial work. I grew up, the years swiftly passing round the London Transport merry-go-round – me, Mum and Dad in our world.

Sherri worked in a big store, sorting out and writing price tags. Life went on. My aunts said they worked in factories. Mum now repaired clothes for a laundry. I never knew what kind of work the aunts did. Later, I heard they were hospital cleaners.

'Necessity!' said Aunt Julie. 'Marvella is facing Necessity. She is twenty-five and no man, no marriage in sight!' My aunt Julie was something special, Everything about her *saw* – her eyes, her face, her hands, her feet. Her whole body saw and said, or had to say.

'You know what that means?' said Aunt Mavis in a considered tone. 'It means we have not had a family wedding for twenty-five years. Marriage would be good for her. She's in her prime.'

'Wait here!' Dad cut in. 'Wait here! If my girl wants to marry she will. If she don't, she won't.'

I thought it was time I said something. They were talking about me as if I were an absent, deaf nonentity. I cleared my throat and they all looked in the direction of the sound.

'I am not bothered. God leads people into marriage. You say so yourselves, many times a day. Besides I do have a bloke, an admirer, one of the deacon-trainees. He asked me out. Tonight. You know Carlton Springle.'

'That brisk, busy boy who always wear white shirts?'

They settled into their seats, their ears flapping like banana leaves in the wind.

'Where are you going?' asked Dad.

'To a concert, to hear a choir. At St. John's Church. They're singing Gospel.'

I went to the cinema with Carlton Springle a couple of times. What a persistent pest the trainee deacon turned out to be! He chose the darkest corners of the cinema in order to prove his manhood. Accepting his date gave him, or so he thought, a season ticket to my person. I was furious at his prowling hands and eventually walked out and went home. A tentative, half-hearted apology, and he was back. Grinning from ear to ear and cooing like a turtle dove hell-bent on mating, he said, 'Don't frighten, Marvella. Don't frighten. I'll use a condom. After three dates, it's time.'

'Look you, mudhead. Don't you understand anything? You could use a golden condom with a £50 note on it and it would never be time for me and you. You twopenny dump!

You come on like *A High Wind in Jamaica*!' (I had been reading that book.)

That clarified our position. He ignored me thereafter. I stayed home, growing old with my family. I began to imagine that my joints creaked each morning. I began to worry.

Sherri and I took our vows of purity, as one was expected to do as a member of our Church. We were determined to say no to premarital sex whatever the pressures. Sherri left her job and went to Teacher Training College in South London.

Another year passed. I was twenty six — set for the shelf with my shelf-life diminishing daily. Mavis sympathised with me. 'You're so beautiful,' she said. 'Tall and slim with a round, inviting backside, yet man never notice you. You too pick-pick. Pick-pick gal never eat bellyful, never get fat. Pick-pick gal, janey-bamboo gal!'

'Well, I just can't accept anybody. I just don't meet anyone suitable.'

She pushed *Westindian World* towards me. 'Look, they advertising for chaps.'

My eyes wandered down the page. The advertisers certainly weren't shy. *Ample Black beauty needs doting tolerant male for serious fun, dancing, theatre, jazz concerts.*

'I'm still young enough to pick,' I replied angrily. 'All you're thinking about is the dressing up and the ceremony. *You* advertise! *Over-forty-two-year-old needs wedding to attend. Could be her own.*'

After that she left me to my own choices. None of which came to anything. Despair, no matter how amorphous, no matter how tenuous, was catching, and my Aunt Julie noticed that I had lost my *joie de vivre*.

'You look depressed,' she said. 'Something will give. I am going home to see to some business on my dead husband's side. You want to come?'

To Guyana! Things were bad there. Poverty, no foreign exchange. Many of the hopes of independence had collapsed. I declined, but she was going all the same.

But Aunt Julie did not give up so easily.

'My friend in Guyana has a son called Ansel,' she said confidentially. 'She is dead now and he is an only child, living with the father. You want to correspond with him? If you want, I'll ask him to write. He must be around your age. I did promise the father to look out for some nice girls to write to him. None I know nicer than you. My niece, level-headed and kind. Coming from our family is a good start.'

'We'll see,' I replied and left the matter at that.

While she was away, I filled in for her at the Church. I worked with Mr. Davidson, a quiet, self-important, elderly man who wiped his mouth with swift strokes of a handkerchief as white as a rabbit's tail-puff, every time he spoke. His whole life had been the church. He spoke of it as a dear friend. I also met Mr. Jones, who smiled broadly at any mention of my solid dependable Aunt Julie. She *was* thorough, whatever mode she assumed, whatever role she played. Later, as their friendship grew, it was fun to watch them, pretending to be young, flirting and making cow's eyes at each other.

Full of smiles and schemes and carrying sentimental objects from Guyana, my Aunt Julie returned safely. My parents were delighted. Auntie talked of how things were looking up for black people in the country, in spite of the hardships, and said she was seriously thinking about returning home as soon as she could. My godmother, Sherri's mother, whom I called Auntie Monica, was present and looked sad, while the others laughed and joked. Suddenly she burst into tears.

'Wha' wrong?' asked Dad, hugging her.

'Yes, wha's wrong. Sherri pregnant?'

'Don't be so stupid. Is all you can t'ink about? Sherri going to be a nun. She got one more year's training to do and she leaving it to be a nun.'

'A nun — a bride of Jesus. She decide?'

'And you crying? It's good. She will never have the worries of children, husband, family,' said Dad.

'What else is a woman for? Truly for?' My aunts still lived in the Middle Ages. I remember their discussion on our prospects. Sherri was to be a woman and I a wife. 'Some day Marvella will make some man a good wife.' And now life was proving them wrong. Sherri evidently wanted to be neither.

Fate is like a wheel that turns slowly enough to allow interruptions, twists, turns, explosions and simple, or mysterious occurrences. An air letter arrived for me.

I hesitated. I could think of no one I knew in the land of my birth who wished to write to me, but curiosity got the better of me and I tore the letter open, though only after a struggle, so firmly was it sealed. It was as if the sender expected every postman en route to be inquisitive. A nosey-parker.

> La Repentance Village
> Guyana

> Dear Miss Marvella Payne,
> My letter will surprise you, but I hope it is a good one and you will be pleased about it. Some time ago I met your aunt, Mrs. Wilmot, and she gave me your name as somebody who would correspond with me and show me something of the world beyond, albeit only in the pages of a letter.
> I am twenty-seven years old, a member of our Church, and have pledged my faith for seven years. I work at the Rice Marketing Board. I went to school

to secondary stage and passed my exam with sixty percent. I like cricket, fishing and running. If I get the chance I can run all day.

My mother passed away two years ago and I live with my father, a lay preacher. I am hard-working, quiet and hope to do well.

To be honest, Miss Payne, a great urge comes over me to change my life by marriage, to a reasonable lady and fulfil the Lord's commandments to be fruitful and multiply. I don't go round writing people, but I ask Miss Monica about you, and Miss Ella, my father's cousins, and they gave you a good character.

So please write to me, Miss Payne. You sound a really nice young lady and I am curious about knowing your heart and other parts.

Respect from
Ansel McKay.

I decided to withhold the information from my family and did not reply just then. I wanted to discuss the letter with Sherri before I replied, if at all, but the older family members always seemed to be around. But now, looking back on my life, I could say that it was at that moment that the long countdown to love began for me, with the man who would eventually become my husband.

Sherri was my best friend. She had been left in the care of her grandmother in Guyana and joined her mother in London when aged thirteen or fourteen. When I was in junior school, she was in the secondary school and was warned to look after me. She had always been my confidante. Before too long we met in the chemists by lucky accident. She had run out of nail polish, her one indulgence.

'Think back to your Guyana days,' I said. 'You remember a boy called Ansel McKay?'

'Yes. He was two classes below me. He's your age.'

'He want me for pen-friend, ha-ha-ha.'

'Well he's OK! A bit country. No hot rod but OK. Respectable. He always wore a shirt and tie. And the boys used to call him that, 'Shirtantie'.'

'What he looks like?'

'Berry-brown skin, big nose, tall, curly hair and a kind nature. Once he had a pet calf. And it died. He cried. He had a funeral. We all went. All the children. He got sympathy. Heaven knows how he still single! A hundred must have tried and failed.'

'He's like us, pledged to chastity before marriage!'

'Must be hard for the poor chap. I bet they think he's queer. These chaps over there go hunting, pledge or no pledge. They have to prove. Manhood! Skankin! Do it! Do it! Do it!'

'What should I do? Shall I write back?'

'Well, he can't seduce you by letter so *I* would. He's OK. Plenty land. Nice preacher father and aunts. Come to think, the father is a bit like old Mr. Jones — respectable, constant like night and day.'

I felt as if I was no longer dropping into a chasm after talking to Sherri. I replied to the letter with a merry heart. What stuck in my head was the mention of land. I respect land. It is the earth.

Dear Mr. McKay,

You must admit your writing is hard to read as it took me three weeks to really read your letter. You will be my first ever penfriend. I had always thought of writing to a magazine like *Essence* or *Ebony* or *Jet* for a penfriend but never really got round to it. I am 27 and work as a typist for London Transport in the local office. I am five foot six, which is tall for a girl. I like to do exercises like swimming and walking. I sew and knit and cook. I go to carpentry classes and pottery. I read. I am not one for going to discos. I am a home-body. As you know, our Church is strict and my life has no high points, no fireworks. I have both my parents. Like you, I am an only child, cared for by two aunts as well as Mum and Dad, who is a master-carpenter and works for British Rail. I go out with my workmates to respectable places.

I have lived in England since I was three, in this lively, racially-mixed part of London.

I hope this little bit of correspondence will be of sufficient interest to you, so that you feel you can continue to write. I like getting airmail, but please don't seal them so tightly. There are no 'letter-peepers' in the P.O. here.

Sincerely,
Marvella Payne

I read my letter over the phone to Sherri.

'Not a word of love?' she chided.

'A respectable girl does not show her hand.'

'Go right out and post it before you change your mind.'

I thought my letter was to the point. Beckoning but reserved. I posted it, with a duty-done feeling. My imagination took over. I dreamt of assignations and disappointments with them. I dreamt of being chased and swallowed up by whales and gobbled by sharks. Each one looked like a person I knew. Both sharks and whales!

All this disturbed my usual equilibrium and I confess that I was being perpetually short-tempered. At length I broached the subject when we were all seated round the food. The high point of our day.

'Who's been giving out my address to all the inhabitants of Guyana? Some kind of "tricky tranny, obeah granny" ruction?' I ended my question like Mum.

'What sort of question that? What do you mean, all the inhabitants? You know how much people that is?' That was my dad.

'Is me she getting at? I gave her name to Bebe McKay son to get her a penfriend,' Julie admitted.

'You might have asked me first,' I snapped.

'No harm intended,' said Julie. 'I was over there I saw the young man. I thought him nice. I struck when the iron was hot.'

'You ought to thank your aunt,' Dad said in a half-joking, half-serious manner. 'She had your interest at heart.'

I suppose my father was right. I sat turning the pages of *Sons and Lovers* while they discussed the McKays. The men died young. The women went on forever, except of course for Bebe, who had come into the family. Being half-Amerindian and half-African she had, they said, a 'weak' side. I felt a deep pity for my penfriend and waited anxiously for his letter. After what seemed like years it arrived. Not an airletter this time but a real letter. Thick and impressive. I hurried to my bedroom and in the stillness I read the missive.

Dear Miss Payne,

Thank you for your sweet and precious reply in such a pretty handwriting. You must have had a good teacher. You sound a really homely type but you must be able to enjoy things, not only obey Church rules. God made the earth to be for each of us as 'a little garden'. A great wave of happiness swept over my face as I read, and perhaps one day in the near future, I will be able to see you face to face. Work is plenty at the moment as it is the rice harvest and the crops are coming in. I go home late, sometimes to an empty house, sometimes to my father. I read your letter again and then my other papers etc. and then

17

put myself in the hands of my maker to sleep. My dreams are very sweet. You figure in all of them and I am content. I am feeling happier by the day. Please write me soon again, Miss Payne. Can you remember anyone here? The old people remember the family and say you were just a chit with ribbon bows when you left. My kind mother died two years last week and we kept a little service here to remember her. My father is happy to have a public remembrance again. Now she can be left to rest in peace. The holiday season is upon us. School soon close and the children will be out swimming and playing cricket. They will soon forget who the cat run away with and be dunce when they go back to school.

All the best, Miss Payne. Please send me another beautiful letter.

Respect,
Ansel McKay

The nosiest woman in the world is my Aunt Mave. Marriage for me was still regarded as a necessity and she would find quotation after quotation from the Bible to support her views. The door of my room swung open and the smell of 4711, a cologne she always used, wafted in.

'When you die I'll smell your jumbie,' I said.

'Sweet thing,' she cooed in her pseudo-Yankee voice. 'How is that letter writing treating you, girl. Any progress?' She had gone to America years ago for ten days.

'Nothing to tell. We're still just penfriends.'

'How many letters fly backwards and forwards?'

'Don't know. A few.'

'Make hay while the sun shines. Tell him he got a rival. Torture him.'

'Is that what you did?'

'Don't worry 'bout me.'

'And Mr. Davidson. Is there a Mrs. Davidson?'

'There must have been. The old man keeps saying, "Mavis I loves you". But what is love? I want someone to show me life.'

I laughed. 'Dad says is what you live with your partner.'

'I know what love is,' she said. 'Love is saying do this, or do that as often as possible, saying not tonight as often as possible, buying what you want and being selfish and complaining.'

'You are talking about being controlling, time wasteful and childish,' I snapped. 'You're not giving me good advice. Are you happy, aunt? Content with your lot?'

'I was once. Till the fool drowned himself. I am lonely wherever I am. Marriage for young girls is necessary. Then you can be a mother when you mean to be one. See you get married, hear me! I spelt out unhappy love for you, the kind I know.'

She was weeping. I had always thought her strong and incapable of any weakness. She had never before showed vulnerability. I knew then that what I had previously taken for strength was loneliness and guilt. I understood the forays she made into the 'country', her response to the more than fatherly touches by Mr. Davidson, the secret looks and gestures between them. She, too, was counting down to love, but for a slippery eel who kept hiding more and more behind the rocks of business, work and preaching.

Every now and then, however, he took her off to some haven where the Church of the Holy Spirit was unknown. She found her double life a strain. Every day of her life, my youth and my life reminded her of the tensions in her own. Whatever she did, or resolved, Mr. Davidson turned to his own advantage. Poor, poor Aunt Mave!

She had, she said, been engaged for eight years to a bright young man from the town. He knew how to be smooth and sweet-talking, and lost his job when the girls took him over.

He took to fishing. One day he did not return. They had been married for a few short months. He was drowned, face down in the water.

Aunt Julie had better memories, bunches of letters tied with blue ribbon. She read them when she was down and locked them away carefully again. However, since her love for Mr. Jones, they had become less important.

I had never written love letters in my life and doubted that I would be able to sustain a correspondence over a long period. Writing calls for stamina. That was not something I knew myself to have, worse luck. Anyway the die had been cast. There was no turning back, not intentionally. I began to notice young couples sitting so close, a breath of air unable to pass between them, their wedding rings shining new. Not much later the baby came along, the mother nubbling endearments into its cheeks, under the delighted gaze of the father. But I wanted my future plainly laid out before me. If only I could have glimpsed it, noticed the contours, felt the texture, but who knew where hopes began or where they ended.

I confided in my workmate, Maria, who shared a desk with me. She was most sympathetic.

'I know just how you feel. When I was having all that hassle and that, with my Winston not wanting to get engaged, what did I do? I went straight to visit Madam Rasia, the famous gypsy fortune-teller. She's really, re-ea-eally famous and can see into the deepest depths of a person. Even animals. She talks with them. And now here I am flashing my ruby and zircona ring.'

I made a face. One of Mum's West Indian specials.

'It's orright for you to do that, but go and see her. It won't hurt you. She don't bite.'

The suggestion took root, and a few days later, pleading 'urgent family business', I sought out the good lady at a site in Edmonton, although I had always believed in divine providence and prayer. But as Maria said, 'Santa Claus, tooth fairies, duppies and angels all have to help out when you're looking for love' — or was it man-hunting?

I had a job finding the place, but did so at last. It was a strange combination of grass and pebbly earth, pools of stagnant water and heaps of smoking rubbish. Animals and humans freely associated. The men wore caps and expressionless faces. The children touched the animals with gentle hands. I asked for Madam Rasia. They pointed me to a caravan at the far end of the field. It was attractively painted in dark blue and cherry. Attached to the door was a silver-coloured horseshoe to serve as the knocker. I gave a timid knock.

'Yus,' said a voice. 'Come in. I ain't bolted.'

And with one step I was in the presence of the great lady, who smiled a broad welcome. She had no front teeth. The same moment that I noticed their absence, she recalled that she had them in her pocket and hurriedly pushed them into her mouth. Her face was spectacularly white, like a Geisha girl's, only she had covered hers with spots, surely made with the tip of a soft red lipstick.

I sat in what she referred to as the best chair in the house. She looked me over.

'I know why you come,' she said sweetly, and then suddenly getting into the spirit of the thing, shifted her voice a gear or two and almost sang, 'You want to get married! And with a little bit of help from me you will!'

'I came for a reading,' I replied.

'What will you 'ave? Palm, runes, Tarot cards, playing cards, hedgehog bones or crystal? You have to choose. Gie yusself a minute or two.' She disappeared, giving me time to look over the place. It was as neat as wood shavings and as clean as a pip. She returned wearing a shawl with mystical signs printed all over it.

'Have you chose?'

I was not very good at choosing after always having had everything chosen for me. The ball of crystal seemed like a ball of ice, something familiar to me, so I said, 'Crystal, please.'

'I knew you was going to say that,' she chortled. 'You're a crystal person. It's writ all over your face. Now cross my palm. A tenner.'

I paid without a word. She put the note in her pocket with a safe shove and then, withdrawing her hand, gave the little pocket a friendly pat.

The word con-artist came into my mind.

'*Think* what you want to know, love,' she instructed. 'Concentrate.'

She began to wave a hand in squares and circles over the ball of ice and then joining her hands to form a butterfly she began to wiggle all of her fat sausage fingers in line with my eyes. At the same time she breathed and moaned while I concentrated for all I was worth on nothing at all.

''Elp me,' she strained. 'Concentrate. Whatever I do, you concentrate.'

'I am. I am.' I managed to whisper.

'Show your truth,' she commanded the crystal. It must have shown something. But before she could tell me, a piping voice yelled, 'Grandma Rasia, Da said he going to the bets naw. Gie us the dosh.' She ignored him and went on peering into her crystal but when he yelled for the third time, her nostrils working like bellows with rage, she yelled back. 'You Jack Rabbit, you daftee! Didn't I tell you not to come 'ere when I'm working. Cut! You 'ear! Cut!'

I was going to object but my voice floated out of my throat.

Silence. She began to tell me, 'There is an oldish man intrestid in you, love. He is on the way. But there is difficulties facing you. With help from me you will over-power them. There is a beautiful wedding dress hanging over you and we will have to make sure you wear it. And about this man. Do not heed his talk. He is a snake in the grass waiting to get his fangs into you. And...'

Carlton Springle, I hurriedly thought. A snake to be sure. But young.

Another voice outside. Gruffer and more insistent. 'Rasia! Rasia, you in there? Give us the dosh. Time's getting on.'

'Geroff! You old buzzard, geroff! You 'eard me! You buzzard! Coming ere with your mouth full of wind!'

She smiled weakly. 'That's all today, love. See you again, soon.'

'I will have to think about that,' I whispered to myself. But she overheard me. 'No pleasing some,' she countered.

Two days later Maria quizzed.

'Seen Madam Rasia yet? I'm a real addict, I am.'

'All I can say is that I am not, and will never be, a fan.'

Maria seemed hurt by my displeasure with Madame Rasia and began to defend her and her wonderful achievements, but I would not be drawn and slipped away to the coffee machine. She eagerly accepted the coffee I brought back and began talking about a film she'd seen the previous night. It was Indian – full of dancing and singing by women dressed in clinging silk. Winston had liked that. She offered to show me the head-movements.

I smiled and continued to type.

'I hate word-processors,' she said suddenly. 'They smell!'

CHAPTER TWO

Sherri had gone to her retreat where she was learning to become a Christian Worker. She did not seem interested in my pen-friendship, so without anyone else to fill me with horrid doubts and analyse and interpret every word of the letter I had received, I replied at once.

> Dear Ansel McKay,
>
> It seems to be taking me a long time to read your letters. Can you guess why? You make me want to hide myself when you describe my simple letters as the cause of so many pleasures. I can promise that your penfriend is a simple person, thought quite odd by her workmates, because she does not go to discos but to the theatre, to concerts and to the Covent Garden shopping-centre to look at the new shops, and watch the street-theatre in the summer. London is a big town. It cannot be imagined. When you come here everything changes — the view you take of yourself and the view you take of the world, of people and what you believe. The simpler and stronger your belief, the harder it is to fit in, since so many people believe in nothing. Not even in love. Love is for many young people pleasure in the company of another. It could change without notice.

Having you as a penfriend would let me imagine the life I would live if I had remained in Guyana.

My cousin Sherri is going to become a missionary and work in Africa. She wants to help and give up her life to service. Unlike me, she does not want to be a wife and a mother and grow old along with a man of her choice. I shall miss her but I will have two penfriends. All my family are well.

You sound much older than you are and perhaps wiser too. Am I the only penfriend you have or are you one of those collectors of people? You must let me know. It is nice receiving letters from people who are distant and unknown. You can imagine them and draw them or paint them and hope you will recognise them should you meet them.

Sincerely,
Marvella Payne

Too many 'thems' I thought. But no matter I won't change a word.

Mum said, 'You seem happier these days. Let's go down the market and see what's what. I need some new sheets.' Just as we were out of the gate, who should appear but our postman! I rushed up to him and blurted out, 'Anything for me?' I saw the startled look on Mum's face, and she noticed the disappointed expression on mine. He informed me that Mondays and Thursdays were the days when overseas mail was delivered.

'You expect to hear from that boy again?' Mum asked.

I nodded. 'He's my penfriend. No harm, is there?'

'I remember love,' Mum said. 'It was like a fire in my heart. It use to blaze up when I saw your Dad. He had the sweetest smile. His eyes and his smile said everything. We used to walk on the sand and told me that one day, some wonderful day, we would fly to a place where stars are as deep as the ocean, and we would play in it like two children. The happiest day of my life was not our wedding service but when I came to rest beside him and everybody had gone home. The night was so quiet. I still can hear him saying, 'Marvina, mine. My Marvina.' I was a truly white bride. Love or no love, don't lose your shame.'

We stood at the bus stop. Silence. Deep silence. I could not speak. I had discovered that my mother had a centre that was soft, that was tender, where beautiful sentiments bloomed and which were fed and watered by her husband.

Ansel's letter arrived on Thursday. By the second post. Mum picked it up from the mat and placed it in my room which my Aunt Mave had arranged in a square-cornered way with the bed in the middle. On the spur of the moment, I decided to rearrange my room. I pushed my bed to the wall, and so gained space for a sitting area. Satisfied, I sat down and, monitoring my actions, opened and read my letter. A photograph fell out. It was amateurish, but it gave a good overall impression of a man who could easily have been an Arab. The nose was high and prominent in an open face. The mouth was sharply incised and the ears well-shaped and flat. All the other features appeared indistinct. He was pleasing to the eye but this was only half of him.

> Dear Marvella,
> Please forgive the liberty. But I can't go on calling my sweet, intelligent penfriend, 'Miss'. I would give you full marks for your wonderful letter. What can I say? I only wish I could fly, or find a magic carpet to put me beside you, Marvella. Is there a chance for something greater than pen-friendship? Every letter you write to me, makes me want to lay my heart at your feet.
> Marvella, I hesitate to ask this question. Am I

the only penfriend you have? If there are more than one of us, I am sure I will lose the battle — a simple man here in a simple country.

I get restless when I think of the distance between us and no chance of us meeting up for years. I grew up in a humble home where pride was said to go before a fall. So I step slowly. Honestly, I would like this friendship to grow and bloom. We have had the same kind of home-training and other things like belief, parents and schooling. When do you think you can let me know if we can expect to find the green fruit of hope, which will ripen into the delicious fruit of love, and place your heart beside my own. I feel in my bones that you will be right for me and when I fall in love it will be for ever.

My father said the moment he saw my mother he knew. He saw her one week and married her the next week and the love between them was a blade of grass that grew into a bush.

Item.	I like your education.
Item.	I like your handwriting.
Item.	You make me laugh.
Item.	We have the same family friends.
Item.	We are suited but we must pray to fall in love.

I send you my sincere appreciation.

Your friend Ansel

Like a limpet he had attached himself to my mind. If I held to my faith, I would trust the Holy Spirit Congregation to pledge their prayers for me. But doubt is a cancer, detaching reality from the ground of belief, growing like a mushroom from a tiny spore into elephants' ears! It did not seem right to pray about love when distrust, like the footsteps of a marauding herd, raised dust clouds that hid the true nature of feelings. Then there were the locusts of fear, destructive of whatever fell into their jaws.

My parents and even Sherri, who knew that clouds of change had settled over my life, were afraid to offer advice — just in case it didn't come right this time. My dad kept a suspicious silence.

Sherri was so occupied with thoughts of famine, flood, raging war and injustice, I never knew which continent she inhabited from moment to moment. The plight of children taken away to become boy-soldiers particularly concerned her. She assumed that they were unhappy. She regarded children as innocent until corrupted by the situations in their lives. She assumed that all feeling, all thinking, all forms of being were set in stone and experienced in the same way by all men and women on earth.

'Why are you making such a meal of this affair?' she said without looking in my direction. 'Whatever will be, will be. Don't work too hard at it. There's nothing to work with. Go there if you must. You're old enough to go back where you came from.'

Later, Mave told me that Sherri's departure to Africa had been deferred for two years. She had to be more thoroughly trained. She must finish her teacher training. Sherri had wept with disappointment. Selfishly I wept with joy. I had the feeling that I had not lost my childish beliefs about keeping loved ones forever. Beside the teachings of my Church about Jesus and his angels, there existed Santa Claus, Hope Fairies and Miracle-workers, all of whom helped me. Underneath all the turmoil of distance there was a tranquil sea. Yet I had to be careful of plunging into it. I wrote.

Dear Ansel,
No I don't mind you using my first name. People here feel free to call everyone by their first

names. I like my friends to use it and you are now one of them. I am surprised that on your check list you like so many things about me. Thanks. I have never had so many compliments from one place. I think you are right about the things which are the same in our backgrounds. But friction starts with things that are not the same. What do you say about that? My parents talk for hours in the darkness of their room until they reach agreement. I remember that when one of my uncles got married, it took off his spirit like a jacket. He was miserable when he was at home with his "inside" wife and put his spirit back on the moment he was outside the house. We must at least pinpoint what are our differences. We don't have to go on to argue about them.

Your photo is not how I imagined you. You are quite good looking! What do the girls nearby think? Have they not the same desire to love and look after you? Are you not yet a child-father? Never mind the pledge. It's the need to prove manhood. Now more news. My cousin Sherri is not going to Africa for a few months yet. She remembers you and the funeral for your calf, that died. She is a hard-working young woman and the sister I never had.

Come September, I hope to start classes in bricklaying.

Bricklayers fascinate me. I stop to watch them working and never cease to admire the skill that they show. The rain has begun again. It is very wet but over here no one bothers about the rain — whatever kind falls. Sometimes it comes down as if it is sieved. It is so fine. Or we may have big or little drops that drum or pitter patter. At other times the sound is like a dog and a cat at war; and then there is the 'argumentative woman' type of rain going on and on.

Mum says the rain over there drum and snortle and snore.

Very best encouragement for a warmer and deeper friendship.

Marvella

I woke early the next day and posted my letter. Over breakfast I thought for the first time about falling in love with someone so far away across the seas. It made me think of other things too — the earth, its mysteries and many nations of people, their characters and the way they showed them. I thought of men, of women and of men and women together. Of our West Indian men, and how they viewed women, first as mothers, and then as partners and then just possibly as wives. How infidelity seemed to be woven into the fabric of their minds, and the chicanery and the deceit that men outside the bounds of our religion seemed to practice. Our strict church taught purity, thrift, moderation and service. It was like a good parent. It taught us to regard both body and mind as wholesome gifts from our Creator. I was happy with that and never envied those girls who became mothers, burdened mothers — their children grandmothered by the social services. Many of my school friends, elated at being called mummy, went out for an encore.

Where was fatherhood in all this?

Ansel was no different, I was sure. Chock-a-block with his own deviances that I could never see. Secrets I would never know. I was burning with unease.

I telephoned Sherri's cousin, Winona, as Sherri would be off to church at that time of the morning. Winona had seen life. She knew a bit about men. She was Sherri's real cousin by her father. I wanted to ask her if sex was all a girl could give. The telephone rang. A sleepy voice and then a deep breath.

'Hey, Marvella. This time a the mornin. Whappen?'

'Oh nothing much! I wanted to ask you — oh, never mind.'

'I worked till eleven last night. It was a good banquet. You never come?'

'No, Winona. I'm a bit worried. A bit depressed. I must make some decisions.'

'Tell you what. Hop by me today — round t'ree o'clock and we will talk. Marian comin' too.'

'OK, Winona. Bye.'

I thought once again of my love-experience — the resistance to prowling hands in the cinema, the detached and tender care of my devoted parents, the constant interference of my aunts and the sisterliness I got from Sherri, all showing only snatches of a reality that matched my own. Uh-huh. That's all I knew! How would I recognise the real thing! The poetry of love. My mere taste of daring about love was expressed in *The Song of Songs*. I read it. I lived it. I learned bits of it by heart. My one adolescent sin. *The Song of Songs*!

'Hark! My beloved! Here he comes,
bounding over the mountains, leaping over the hills
My beloved is like a gazelle
or a young, wild goat!
There he stands, outside our wall
Peeping in at the windows, glancing through the lattice.
(A quick vision of a fine young man at my window and me
in the first stage of undress. My hair untied.)
Rise up, my darling
My fairest, come away
For now the winter is past.
The rains are over and flowers appear over the earth.
The time of the singing birds has come
And the turtledoves cooing will be heard over the land.

Rise up, my darling
My fairest, come away.
I sleep, but my heart is awake
Listen! My beloved is knocking.'

I was by now melting away with desire for something I could not name. It was delicately massaging my viscera. Was this love? Another quick glance into the future. A ring on my finger. Clear as day. It glowed. New gold. Love! Marriage! Me! 'Take me, my darling,' I whispered.

The time of the singing has come.
Open flowers cover the earth.

'Uh-huh,' I said, 'lots of them! Flowers and grass and me lying surfeited with love.'

'You all right in there, Marvella? You all right? You talking to yourself again!' My fifteen year old eyes had been ablaze with the effrontery. *She* had once again intruded into my private moment. I hated my Aunt Mave. Had I the powers I would have turned her into a witch. Once she caught me reading about Lot and his daughters. 'You are wicked!' she yelled. 'The Philistines will come down upon you.' I was terrified of them and sat reading at my desk waiting to be devoured by Philistines — whatever they were. 'Read this. Learn it and inwardly digest it. It's Chronicles. It's good for you,' Aunt Mave said, pushing the open Bible at me. Angrily I read:

'Next day when the Philistines came to strip the slain, they found Saul and his sons lying dead on Mount Gilboa. They stripped him, cut off his head and took away his armour.'

'Your armour will be taken from you, bad girl. Lot's wife — I ask you!' my Aunt said, as I sniffed out the last word.

Dad mercifully released me from these memories when

he called in from the kitchen, 'Come, Marvella, I've brought a surprise.'

A letter had arrived. It was carefully printed for a few lines of the page:

STOP PRESS. MAN TO MEET BELOVED PENFRIEND. SOON.

It continued:

> Dear beloved Marvella,
>
> God is with us. I have been chosen to attend a course on Marketing. I think the place has the name of Oxford Polytechnic. I will be there for four weeks. I am getting prepared. I will be over there in two weeks and three days time. Early November.
>
> I will see you then. Store up all the news but ask your father if he will allow my presence in his home as a visitor. I am respectable and he will have no trouble with me. Sherri Maybee's mother will keep me for a week so I get to know you. Excitement is tearing me up. I am so happy. It is bubbling like mauby bark inside me.
>
> Bestest, brightest love,
>
> Ansel

I gave a little cry — one that a child might utter at the sight of a desired toy or a much loved present from Santa. My aunts dashed in, their faces full of melodramatic concern.

'Whappen?' they said in treble and alto.

'Oh, I was just celebrating my news — screaming a little.'

'You sound as if somebody jook you with a hat pin. Whappen?' My aunts always spoke Creole to show concern.

'Ansel coming. The Government sending him on a course for five weeks — four plus the one to get to know our family. It's so unexpected.'

'I bet his father work it. He's a Mason. Those Masons, they are a bribing brotherhood. I don't trust them,' said Aunt Julie.

'Thank you very much,' I said. 'Thank you for sharing my happiness.'

'What's up with her? The girl so touchous.'

'She want us to climb a wall and bark to show we are glad. Then she happy.'

I closed my door. Their muttering voices came through the keyhole, followed by their eyes if they could have managed it. I can't imagine what they thought I was doing.

Minutes later Dad came home. I did not go downstairs at once so he came up and knocked on my door. Beaming, I showed him the letter.

'I am happy for you, love. Any friend of my daughter is welcome here.'

I nodded. 'Tell Mum,' I said. 'Now I will know for certain. Are you truly pleased, Dad?'

'Don't make too much of your aunts' interference. They mean well. Give over the matter to the One who knows all things. We'll do you proud. We will make this house a welcoming place.'

I had quite forgotten about my promise to stop by Winona. It was well past three o'clock. There was nothing to do but admit my forgetfulness. And there was Sherri to be told about it all, though she was creating a world different from the one we all knew and the bonds that bound us to her were getting looser by the day.

I began planning how to tell people. Sherri's mother, my godmother, would be told by my parents after we met and *if* Ansel and I 'made a match'. Then I realised how foolish I was being. Ansel would be her guest for a week, and they would be bound to talk! When I met Sherri after work she seemed very pleased to see me.

'I wasn't expecting you. It's nice. Thanks for the surprise.' Arm in arm we walked towards a little Italian sandwich bar and sat down. Over a cup of coffee I told her of Ansel's impending visit.

'I want him to come, so that I can put my feelings to the test. I have always been told how to be, what to think and say and do. It has made me insecure — unable to decide — afraid of making mistakes.'

'It's what you give out. You have to stop behaving like a shattered woman, a child-woman. Make your decisions yourself. Consider the pros and cons. Then decide. You discuss too much. You hand each of us a little spoon and you let us stir. Don't do that when he's about. Be competent. He wrote to Mum but I forgot about it.'

I felt very upset at Sherri's words.

'The times are changing,' she continued. 'I'm sorry you're upset, but it's true. Auntie Monica, Mave and Julie have had their lives. This is yours. When opportunity knocks, it's how you answer. Do battle for what you want.'

She sat beside me and took my hand. Stroking my fingers she added in a lofty, crimson voice, 'Modom, I can assure you, every one of these 'ere fingers should be covered with diamantine.'

We laughed, silly girls that we were.

'You know, my mum *is* a provocation. She tells everyone, I'm going to be a nun,' said Sherri petulantly on the way home. 'I am not. I want to be a missionary. Mum thinks that I am going to force people to do what they don't want to do. I want to work in a community — teach, help, serve. Sometimes I could bite into her. Vampire her to make her listen to me.'

We giggled like children.

'I'll talk to her. Tell her how to describe you. Call you a missionary instead of a nun.'

'Don't, Marvella. Not in my presence at least. The less the family knows the better.'

'You're right,' I said. 'Be careful of the leaves on the pavement. They cover over the dung from these over-fed canines round here. They drop dung anywhere.'

The pavement was covered with leaves. No sweepers had come round for ages. Autumn was in the air. The birds were migrating. Different patterns and different sounds high above the earth. How did they know their time?

After Sherri had gone home, I wrote to Ansel.

My dear, true Love,

What happy news you have sent me! I am delighted to hear of your prize, for that is what it surely is. I will at last be able to meet you in the flesh not as pen-friend but as person. It is getting very much colder, especially in the morning when it is so misty it looks as if the whole world is covered over with gauze. When the sun comes out, the mist disappears and Sherri and I go about on the Heath which is like a big, wild park with tall trees. Now they are shedding their leaves and the branches look like long, bony fingers pointing to the skies.

It would be a real surprise to be able to hear your voice and to put a sound to your good looks. I think, although you may not agree with me, that a man is like his voice and a woman like her imagination, especially when she is hoping for wonderful things to happen.

My father has a most interesting voice. It runs on ahead of him like a river with friendly windings in it. I find myself thinking a great deal about you, and wondering what you will think of me. I am quite attractive. My room is full of my personal things and I would be pleased to show them to you. Have no fear, and be sure that you will be an honoured guest in our home.

Love to you and all those you hold dear,
Marvella

We got the house ready.

Mum and my aunts thought of the house as having a special importance, conveying a hidden message to visitors from afar. Perhaps the way the house was arranged was seen as having invisible powers to unite or divide and to affect both consciousness and affinity in special ways. The chairs were undressed and the covers cleaned and replaced. The curtains, too, came down. Professionals came to clean the flowery carpets. Artificial flowers that could not be washed were replaced. Dad bought a new punch set as the old one was chipped. My aunts bought new plastic curtains for their room and a variegated array of fake velvet cushions from Woolworths – orange, green, red, gold. Our house was a black West Indian working class house. My parents' house. The prototype for mine. I counted the days. Ten more — six more. Four more and then the day dawned.

'I can't go to meet that boy on Sunday morning. I must have my rest,' said Dad.

The women pleaded church. I was left holding the baby.

'I'll come with you,' offered Sherri.

'No. What ever's to come I'll face alone.'

I was saved from interference and that had given me extra strength. I believed in the power of sharing time, which is a mystery. We can or cannot spare it, we have it or don't have it, we use it throughout life but we do not really know where time comes from and where it goes. Mmm. Those were my thoughts and my aunts always warned me about them. 'Watch your thoughts like you watching an unruly child. Hold on tight to your thoughts'.

CHAPTER THREE

It was one of the those classic November mornings, frosty and foggy with a persistent ice-cold drizzle, like a crying baby that could not be comforted. I went by coach to Heathrow and arrived half an hour before the flight touched down. Disembarkation and Customs would probably take another three-quarters of an hour. Even though I was well-wrapped up — winter coat, boots, warm hat and gloves, I felt the cold. I stood right in front clutching the barrier. He could not possibly miss me. Rapidly I looked around. A good few girls my age waited for friends, relatives or like me, for a penfriend. I wore my red hat, velvet, trendy and new. I wasn't the only red hat.

I saw him lumbering out, clutching what is called in Guyana a portmanteau, a small suitcase, a sodden cloth bag and other bits and pieces under his arm. He had thought neither of climate nor of seasons. Dressed as for a summer's day, except for his felt hat, his flimsy, brown lightweight suit, an inch or two too short in the legs, was splattered with raindrops, just as one sprinkled starched clothes in the old days before ironing them. He caught sight of me and smiled broadly. His face was like finely carved African wood, his nose like a cashew. I was so engaged by his face, his height and the hat, that I forgot about the clothes, though I quickly noticed that he had not worn an overcoat.

'Marvella? Marvella?' he asked nervously, holding out a shivering ice-cold hand. 'You just like you photo.'

'Yes,' I replied. 'You must be cold. Did you think you were coming to the same hot climate?'

'No, not at all! Not at all! You can't buy clothes such as yours over there. I have money to buy what I need. I had no time. I couldn't postpone my chance to travel to the land of knowledge...'

'You must be freezing. Come, I'll get us some tea.'

'I can't drink tea too hot. I drink it cold.'

'Well, chocolate then. Something to warm you through. I'm sure you're freezing. You're not a tropical man any more.'

Just at the entrance there was a booth selling warm drinks and we found two seats and sat drinking chocolate like old friends.

I caught sight of him eyeing me, taking my full measure without any kind of expression that I could evaluate. He seemed to be matching the me he had mentally constructed with the me beside him. At last he got the images and the words in the right order.

'Marvella, you're everything I thought you would be. A nice, nice girl. Young, fresh and beautiful to look at.'

I laughed. 'Flattery! Flattery! Won't get you dinner!'

'I mean every word. I'm not just talking through my hat!'

That hat. The grey trilby with the black band. A half-good match for the brown suit with trousers flapping around those long skinny legs and those boats for shoes. What would Sherri say? And Winona, Marsha, Sylvie and the 'Church Ladies'. He was what my mates would call a real yokel from the sticks! Never mind that. He was good-looking and easy to be with. As for the clothes, they were nothing that a visit to 'Tall Boys' could not cure. The sooner we got him into some jeans and a smart padded jacket, the better.

'You'll be staying at my godmother's. My family will

greet you and after you've had a rest, Dad will drive you over. It's not far.'

We gathered up his things and went to wait for the coach. We were the only two people at the stop. He was indeed tall — six foot and over, but his slim build made him appear even taller. I found myself looking up at him and realised that his eyes were a clear brown in colour. When he at last raised his hat, I saw that his hair line had begun to recede. One day, my husband or not, he would be bald.

We spoke little on the way home. The connections we had made in our letters were pretty tenuous. There were vast areas of ourselves, our interests, our likes and our dislikes to be exposed and explored. But the initial contact was good. I liked him and it was up to him to show me what he was truly made of. He was on my territory. I knew the rules.

My parents greeted us at the door. Mum took one look at him and winked at me.

'The good shops are shut,' she remarked, in a tone which was carefully without any hint of criticism or ridicule. 'It's a pity, but tomorrow not far off. Don't worry about clothes.'

'He isn't dressed for the winter,' Mave whispered. 'Someone should have told him.' She showed him to the bathroom.

'Food ready. Come sit down,' Mave called. 'Look,' she whispered to Julie, 'rain drizzle on his crotch-piece.'

I heard him 'washing his hands' and then he came out smiling, a dazzle of white teeth.

We sat down. Mum and Dad at the head and the foot of the table, my aunts on either side of Mum, and Ansel on Dad's right as the guest; I sat on the left.

I said the prayer and we fell on the food. We were all hungry. After a while, we talked. People asked questions and Ansel answered as best he could. He had a clever way with words, a good sense of folk-humour and a clever blend of horse-sense and education. It made a change from the fumblings, verbal and otherwise, of Carlton Springle. Ansel told us all about the hardships of Guyana, the shortages and the decreases in the value of the dollar. 'Everything difficult now,' he said. 'But I will never change from feeling that it can still be the best place in the world to live. God is still there with us,' he concluded.

The meal was a success and we left my father and Ansel to 'discourse'. This is a special speech form — discoursing. It consists of probing questions, arguments and analysis. It is candid talk. And no messing. I knew that my dad, on my behalf, would probe Ansel to his backbone about his finances, his present status, and his future prospects — just in case he married his daughter.

At six o'clock the discourse ended and after a brief handshake, Dad drove him to my godmother's place.

All night, I lay awake thinking, thinking. My heart pounded against my breast like a poco-drum. Now that I had seen him, what? I imagined him out of those clothes but could not imagine him in anything else — except his birthday suit! He was compromised but struggled to restore his respectability by twisting his legs round and round and round. I quickly blinked that one away. Where had this fantasy hopped from? Aunt Mave would have said it was the devil's work, I'm sure. After that I was too tired for further capers and slept so late I had to report sick for work.

I rang Sherri. Before I could say a word she started to laugh. 'You got a case on your hands!'

'What you mean by case? What's wrong with him?'

'Nothing. He's a nice guy.'

'You mean it?'

'Yeah, ha, ha ha. Those legs, ha ha. That suit, ha ha. La, that hat. But he's nice. He talks sense. He's going far! Very far!'

'I like him, Sherri, I really do.'

'He kiss you yet?'

'You mad? He hasn't asked me yet. He talked to Dad, but the questioning is tomorrow. I will tell him I like him and when they start on me, I'll say yes too. So it's all settled.'

'He's full of beans. I'm taking him to 'Tall Boys' for the complete gear — Concept Man. He's nice looking.'

'Thank you, Sherri,' I replied absent-mindedly. 'I'm off work for the day, but I'd rather leave you to do the make-over.'

'Don't you want to dress your man?'

'No thank you,' I said, as an errant vision hopped back into my head.

Being in Britain had evidently emboldened Ansel. True to her word, Sherri had evidently taken him to the outfitters. A yokel had been transformed. I was stunned. It was like walking down a dark forest path and then emerging into a glade of golden light where one tall young sapling stood straight and wonderful to see.

No longer the shy man of yesterday, he greeted Mum and my aunts and then asked me for a few words in private.

Mum nudged my aunts and aunt nudged aunt. Then sniggering like the ladies at a parson's tea-party they left us alone.

'Marvella, if you like me and think you can spend your life with me, I am willing. Are you willing?'

I thought for a moment and then nodded.

He fumbled a large hand in his jacket pocket, produced a box and took a ring from it.

'If you accept this, I will try to make your world full of good things and quiet peaceful times, without worry and, God help me, without want. There will be trials and tribulations, but we'll come out of it if we work as one.'

Mum walked in and we showed her the ring and she

informed the aunts. Dad had known all about the proposal and the engagement. We kissed for the first time. It was the real thing — giving and receiving love again and again. His kisses were warm, wet and lingering and full of the very essences of our hopes and our dreams.

Because of the distance and the red-tape, we would be married in a year's time at the earliest. We had both been saving, but getting money in and out of Guyana was troublesome. Now, though, we set that problem aside and concentrated on the present.

I did not see him again until after work the next day. He was now a regular guy — fashionable and handsome. I was proud of him — his open laughter, his broad twang and his quaint sayings and mannerisms. Those I thought would scoff were complimentary about him. I heard, 'He would make a good model.' 'Look at those shoulders.' The hat had become a cap. He looked so imposing, I was sure some heads turned as we passed by.

We took him to Covent Garden and for the first time in his life he saw white people who were poor. He was fascinated by the sights and the shops, the piles of litter, the November grime, the people like ants everywhere. He braved the cold and the rain to do touristic things and I was able to steer and counsel him.

Even as an old-fashioned girl, I knew that from the moment of my engagement I had entered a new stage in my life. Because I had never been adventurous in my dealings with men, the alphabet and grammar of love were a new language to me. I had to learn it quickly — and in the face of tumultuous feelings of certainty and uncertainty.

Although Ansel was now close enough to touch and cling to, I still felt better writing to him and sharing my happiness with paper.

My darling man,

So beautiful and kind, I write from the green arbour of our new found love. I can see it clearly, a little bud, bright and shining that will grow into a magic flower that will always bloom, and never, never lose its petals. If what I feel is love, then I am all for it. I crave it and embrace it. Mark my words: Love is patient and kind and without envy. Without love I am as a sounding gong or raucous symbols such as I hear in Oxford Street. Love is never boastful nor conceited. It keeps no score of wrongs but smiles at what is right. There is nothing love cannot face. There is no limit to love's faith, which I hope will help ours, never to come to an end. I send you love and all it contains.

Marvella

With a deep loud sigh, I folded it and put it an envelope. I would give it to him when the right time came.

In the better weather we saw what we could of London and then he left for Oxford Poly. But, only a few hours after his departure, I was consumed with a desire to know how he was settling down in such strange surroundings.

He telephoned the following evening.

'It's so cold,' he said. 'You can't imagine. The rain is ice-water. I can't think. The cold is in my bones.'

'And what of the food?' I managed.

'So, so. A lot of puddings and custard like nose-cold. I'm not used to that. I like fried fish, plantains and that. Our food. Meat is not popular with me — too threadish, especially beef.'

'You're managing the work?'

'Oh yes! The lecturer knows his job. I am learning a lot about organising and promoting. It is a whole new language. A whole new way of presenting a product. Even rice is a

44

product. We used to think of rice as something to eat. Kas-kas. Throw it to the fowls. Rice is a product people must want to buy.' He laughed. 'I'll be a learned man when they're done with me. One day and I know everything.'

I laughed. 'I'll ask Mum what kas-kas means.'

'Careless. You don't know Creole? I'll have to teach you. Tomorrow, I'm going visiting a packaging plant. The people are nice to me. They keep saying, "Mind your head. The Satellites are coming".'

His money was running out, but Sherri's mum had the number. 'I'll call back later.'

He was grasping the chance to learn what would be useful to his country. In the process he had found a new voice, confident and enthusiastic. In that he was ahead of me. Like so many British-born or reared black people, I was in a cultural no-man's land. A limbo of identity. Nothing about me was mine. The Queen, the Flag. The Lord Mayor's Show — I could relate to them but never own them. Deep in my heart I knew they were not really mine. Being born here did not make one English. Englishness was heritage, traditions and cultural ownership, running back through the centuries. The rituals, relationships and the language sepa-rated us, often driving us back towards our parents' culture, which itself I only half understood. Carnival, steelbands and reggae were not really mine, yet they were offered to me as something I should own and allow to float before my eyes like gnats in the summer, to blur my vision. Ansel had no such problems. He knew his identity whether of self or place, or race, or religion. I understood more of what I lacked every time Ansel and I talked. Some young people, in their search for meaning and belonging, took refuge in our church. A black church, an island which we constructed each week, where we praised the Lord with music and song. I understood, too, Sherri's longing for Africa. Perhaps not Africa the place, but that Africa which was stamped into her skin, which made her an outsider and set her apart, set her upon the road that so often led to self-rebuttal and self-hate.

I understood. I took a few days leave to join Ansel in Oxford and savour his company. We walked and talked and I became more and more certain. When I returned to work, the girls crowded round my hand admiring the ring. I felt proud.

He was worth waiting for. I described him yet again and amidst the 'wows' and 'oos' and 'tell me more', Maria's voice came through demanding, 'And what of Little Willie. We want to know. Don't we, gels?'

'Really, Maria. Who is little Willie?' I asked, ignoring the wink-wink, nudge-nudge, snigger-snigger. 'Make no mistake. Bad company is the ruin of good character,' I added with mock superiority.

'Don't start, Marvella! Don't be naïve.' Actually she said 'nave'.

The Manager came in and said, 'I gather congratulations are in order?'

'Thanks, Sir.'

'And who is the fortunate young man?'

'No one you know, Sir. Someone from my birthplace.'

'Well, good luck.'

I felt choked by their good wishes and concern. I excused myself and went to the cloakroom and asked God for clarity and strength. I never thought in terms of the images of God offered to me. My God was mysterious, enclosing all life. I could be guided anywhere, at any time. I knew that with Ansel I would be happy.

I wrote to him. The weather was much better. Cold but bright. Dry and clear as crystal. I felt inspired, approved of, chosen.

'Dear kind, loving man,
I hope you are handling the cold with more

confidence and going for brisk walks across the fields. You are in my thoughts all of the time, like a pleasant tune. I can sing it, hum it, or play it on an instrument in my heart. The girls like my ring, and perhaps find it strange to think of me as engaged. I am glad you enjoy the work and are getting such good marks. My parents, godmother and aunts are pleased and I am proud.

I am starting my bricklaying course tonight. It is mostly theoretical; the practical work comes later. Everyone wants to know what I am going to do with it. It's simply something I like to learn about.

Sherri did a course called 'Electricity in the Home'. We want to be able to help ourselves. I can hear you laughing and saying nonsense. But times are changing.

I would like to visit you in Oxford again. If I catch the eleven o'clock train you'll be able to meet me at twelve thirty.

Mum has made some cakes and savouries which I will bring for you.

Please call me. Your speech is very much like my dad's, slow and wide, open like a river.

Love and a sweet kiss,

Truly
Marvella

Two days later he replied. Why shouldn't he. He was only a few hours away.

Dear Marvella,

What an educated letter you wrote to me. It altered my state of mind and threw my studies out of the window. But I am coping with that. I would not be able to bear not hearing from you. I have not yet got over the welcome, the friendship, and the way your people treated me. And your friends the same. My mother wanted that ring to go to my intended, and it fitted your finger like Cinderella's slipper fitted her foot. You are the one for me.

I watched a little TV last night. A romance. It was a little far-fetched, but the love words were wonderful. I would like to tell you that you are my magic. You change my shape and my thoughts and I enjoy the change.

I went for a walk into the town. The shops are full of goods and the street full of people. So much of everything, Marvella, is not right for one nation to have. So much eggs. Eggs everywhere and so cheap. So much shoes and jeans, clothes and everything. I like to have only as much as I need. The weather is still cold but one day we will be together, giving each other warmth or whatever. I got a B- for my work but my dead mother will want A from me. Now my A1 sweetheart, I must close this letter before I drop to sleep over it. I dream of how I can shovel obstacle after obstacle out of the way of your splendid feet.

See you in my dreams. Your intended,
Ansel

PS: Respect to your family and Sherri. Respect to your boss too.

I read my letter aloud to Sherri. She needed cheering up. The officials of Christian Gospel to People Overseas would not accept her unless she completed her teacher training. She was doing her practice in a convent school nearby. It gave her time to meet me from work and listen to my eulogy of Ansel.

By not mentioning the visit I had proposed, I conjectured

that he approved and the following Saturday I made the journey alone. Imagine my surprise when I turned up there to find that he was nowhere to be seen. After a lot of seeking and searching I found one of the porters at the Polytechnic and was told that the entire group had gone on a day-study course. I was angry that I had not been told but I controlled myself and left all the delicacies for Ansel with the porter.

I returned home in a state. Not only was money wasted but why had he concealed his movements? I decided to sulk, because I was uncertain what other form my vexation should take. He had shamed and insulted his own fiancée by hiding information. He had cheapened me in the eyes of a porter.

Mave was furious with me. She growled, 'All of a sudden you're fussy and hot. You should be quietly sewing, preparing. Not running after the man. He has work to do.'

A week passed. No word from him. Had he broken off the engagement?

'Nonsense,' said Dad. 'He is probably waiting for you to calm down. Besides, there must have been a good reason.'

Good reason or not I began to worry. But I was determined not to call. I'd see who could hold out longest. The tension was hard to bear. My heart asked for the sound of his voice, my arm for his touch. Why hadn't he told me of that stupid visit?

I wrote. Destroyed the letter. Wrote again. A stern reprimand. Critical. Again I destroyed it. My third letter. An apology. No. Who did he think he was?

'Marvella,' Julie counselled. 'Engagement, marriage, children to come: when they happen they give you confidence, make you feel special. But remember, my little girl, who I saw born and help raise, pride goes before a fall.'

I thanked her but insisted that I felt good about my actions.

The days passed. He did not write and I had banned myself from the telephone. I felt angry with the man for creating such a need in me. There should be no secrets between couples in love. When we were penfriends, only words and good writing were involved. Now there were feelings and blame, and the need for eyes and lips and hands.

I pretended there was no need to call upon the Spirit for comfort. He would come round in time. I carried on with my work. A little more pensive and quiet. Less enthusiastic in my talk about marriage. Sherri came to the rescue.

'How are you?' she asked.

'Feeling bad. Wondering if my Maker isn't telling me to keep away from Bamboo-Johnny.'

'Why don't you meet me at the Curry House for lunch? Nothing like a good curry to cure the blues. Meet me there at one o'clock.'

'All right.'

I walked into the restaurant and sat facing Sherri and then a pair of arms teasingly encircled me from behind.

'Ansel,' I shrieked. Heads turned. Implements fell. 'Where you come from?'

'My course ended yesterday. I was so busy. Sorry I didn't tell you about our study visit. I didn't know myself.' It was indeed the end of the month! I hadn't noticed. I felt utterly selfish. He had to work hard for his exams, to uphold the name of Guyana as so many of his countrymen and women had done.

'I passed with full credit and I benefited in a million ways. Everybody was willing to help. As for the lecturer, every time he opened his mouth I learned something. A fine man. A gentleman.'

'You didn't miss me?'

'I did, but first things first. I will always have you, but this course was my big chance to be able to keep you as I would like.'

'Well spoken,' said Sherri. 'Some people don't know their luck.'

We walked through the dark cold afternoon to our house. The food was good. The fire of love had been rekindled. My heart was singing. Faith had returned with its feather duster and the dust of anger and doubt had gone. The perfect parts were in place. Sherri grinned. 'It was the only way to stop you boring me to insanity,' she said.

The next day with Mum and Dad, my godmother and my aunts we planned the wedding. I would buy what we needed, send the receipts to Ansel and he would deposit the amounts in an account in my name, until our wedding. It would take place in Guyana in the following June. We would have been engaged for seven months. My godmother had been engaged for eight years. Marriage, to my godmother, had appeared like the final surrender. She had held out. He married the virgin he had known for ten years. She was twenty-seven, my age, when he finally wed her and then only for a short time. He returned home to the comfort of relatives and left his wife to make her way in London. Some people inherit the feet of runaway slaves.

CHAPTER FOUR

Sherri and I accompanied Ansel to Heathrow. He was not dressed in the flimsy museum-piece brown suit of his arrival. This time he wore jeans, a white tee-shirt printed 'Love Happens', a really smart and colourful jacket and a cap sitting jauntily on his head. He was now a young man of the eighties. Gone, too, were the boat-like shoes. They had given way to fashionable trainers. Where was the yokel now?

We offered him tea to warm him up and, still protesting the heat in it, he sipped it after desperately blowing into it. He hugged Sherri and gave me a long, lingering kiss. He carried a travelling bag, every pocket bulging. He seemed to have managed a little something for all the people in the village by the look of his luggage.

I recalled the young man who had come, still, as it were, holding a rake and scythe in his hand. He would return to village, church, job and his father but nothing would be the same. He had tasted the wasteful culture of a developed country. He had seen the global reality of buying and selling, now called marketing, with its own beliefs and practices and outcomes. The course had dusted his corners, turned out the odd mouse or spider lurking there. I was happy to see him leave so light in step and heart, and truly alight in spirit.

I clutched my heart as he disappeared into the bowels of the departure lounge, and I was left to wonder why this simple man moved me so much and made me so desperate to prove my womanhood.

Work depressed me for the rest of the day but when I got home, Mum and Dad had prepared a surprise meal for me.

'Just a little banquet,' Dad teased. 'To prepare us for the big one coming up soon. Seven months aren't long. I can't believe this is happening. I prayed for this day. May it come quick.' He poured a little medicinal gin in his limeade. The aunts were out. Mave and Mr. Davidson had gone into the country to a retreat and my Aunt Julie was openly spending the weekend with Mr. Jones.

Too embarrassed, Mum and Dad did not comment. But I spent the rest of the meal wondering, between mouthfuls of food, exactly what went on between those two old codgers and their controlling, argumentative ladies of the Holy Spirit. Ah well, 'The older the violin, the sweeter the tune.'

I played some music. Not Soul as usual but the love-ballads of the fifties. My parents sprang to life, humming and singing and recapturing those joyous moments of their youth. That was a happy evening, I mean one we all recognised as being that. For me it exposed a bit of my personal history. My parents were children who had grown up, fallen in love, dreamt of a life together, got married, survived hard times and could not prevent cobwebs from growing in their hair. My feelings got the better of me. I wept.

'Time soon pass,' Mum comforted me. 'Time soon pass. I know. You miss him.'

I let her think what she wanted. It was funny that all of them believed that 'inside' feelings didn't matter. To them, things happened outside them in the world and you either noticed them or you didn't.

Very shortly after, Ansel wrote. He had tested the power knowledge gave. Renewed, he wrote:

My dearest Intended,

Here I am, back in the same old place, thinking of you, and my good fortune that my prayers for a good wife should be answered like this — full to overflowing. The work will change here. Plenty of scope to introduce some new thinking in production and marketing. We want to package rice in an attractive way so people can see it and want it. Give it eye appeal. Change comes slow over here but with patience we will make it. Sherri chose some good things for me because all my friends like them, especially my white cricket shirt. That's what I missed most in England. We play cricket here any time as long as the rain can stay away.

I feel so grateful when I remember how all your family accepted me and your godmother, in particular, treated me like a son.

All the little presents brought back were well appreciated. The London postcards and the peppermint sticks in particular. I forgot to buy myself some novels. It went clean out of my head. I wanted to buy some good writers. Adventure, not brutality like war and sex. I like sci-fiction but the course pushed all that aside.

Thank you once again, my good sweet one, my dearest girl, for all your trouble. Thank you for accepting the hand I offered. I am sure we will live for many years in bliss and harmony. You are always with me. May you never leave me. Things are bad and scarce here, making the years to get brick hard, but with you, every minute of life will be a blessing.

Gratefully your intended,
Ansel

PS: The world is a wonderful place and we are good people blest by God.

I sighed. That man was so special I began to wonder how I had come upon him. I had won him through an angel's raffle for sure. I undressed. In almost twenty-eight years I had never thought of my body as a wondrous work, deserving of either inspection or admiration. It had always been dampened down, ignored, or covered up with clothes. Something to be ashamed of, its God-given bits outrageous. I stood before my mirror and stared at a shapely, nubile woman.

'My body,' I said. 'Me. What I see is what I am. What I see, he will see.' For the first time in my life I was happy with my own dear body, a body that was wanted and loved. 'Isn't life wonderful? Isn't truth sweet?'

If someone, someone with money, power, influence, or even a poor, indigent person, came to me and said, 'Marvella, for a million pounds, can you name the moment when you experienced complete freedom and happiness and ecstasy at being you?'

'Yes', I'd say. 'But not for a million pounds. I would tell you for the pleasure of the moment's recognition. It was the moment when I looked at my body and it looked at me. That moment made me a woman.'

What was the life I lived doing for me? I had been given the guidance of truth and explicit precepts to live by. I had taken them to heart and carried them always with me. But there were those who had so hammered me with such precepts, so terrorised me with them, that they made me suspicious of them. My aunts could always find a suitable proverb, a suitable verse from Nahum or Zephaniah to knock me on the head with to frighten my spirit. Then one or the other would sneak off and savour the devil's breakfast till all the crumbs were gone. I felt angry. That is what change does. One reviews the old life, pushes a finger in the

55

mush and gets angry. Strangely, in the midst of all these confusions I was commended for my efficiency at work. Why was that? I was so involved with my own doubts that I could not be bothered to talk. So I worked and worked.

Time was getting on and I had done nothing about my trousseau. Now I began to collect personal things. Sherri accompanied me shopping sometimes. There was a strike in Georgetown. No mail arrived and it was difficult to telephone. Patience was called for. I died a little at a time, worrying about him. At last normal times returned. I wrote to him.

My dear man,

The time is flying past and everyone has offered to help me. I have bought more or less my personal things and must now turn to our home. We won't start with a full house — just essentials and we will take it from there.

We will wait to buy linens and curtains and things like that when Mum comes over to see how the land lies. The big thing is for us to settle down. I am helping Mr. Cornridge, who lives next door to us, to build a wall. He was surprised to see me use a plumbline. I must say, though, that a hod of six bricks is heavy to carry. A burden.

Sherri passed her exams and is going to be spending two months at the Training Centre. It will take her years to be a missionary. You just can't jump and turn like playing hopscotch.

I still miss you and when I am quiet, I wonder what you are doing, and if you are working hard. Things are changing with the railways. They are cutting costs, laying off men, making them redundant and forcing early retirement on young men. Dad has been there so long, I hope they don't touch him.

All the women are in high spirits. And so am I. Sometimes I can jump to the ceiling when I think of us together in married love. I say these wonderful lines to myself, 'With this ring, I thee wed.' I can't wait to say it with conviction. I am happy, you dearest one. Send me a sweet letter.

All my love and true desires,
Marvella, your own

I always found myself smiling when I had finished writing. There were happy feelings inside my heart. They were warm and they were good. More than that really. Blessed. Work, too, was pleasant. I had now been promoted to becoming secretary to Mrs. Alwyn, a kind lady who told me on our first meeting, 'When I am working, I don't play.' I understood her.

'When *I* am working.' That is all that concerned me. I was in a new section. Hopefully not for long. I met the girls for lunch and they always offered me tit-bits to say to Ansel.

Then Fate took a hand. Another hand I should say. Not a very kind one. My dad had been offered a choice: redundancy or early retirement. My dad was still young and active at 58. To make him redundant would be an attack upon his life, his home, his family. It would be culling bits from all of us. Dad had started in the hard days and worked like a tiger to get on, because of his faith and his self-belief.

Overnight my father changed. His shoulders drooped, his eyes showed fear as he pondered his choices.

'I don't know what they will offer me. I would take early retirement but I might be paid a pittance.'

'Hear what the Union have to say.'

'They fight for their own. Once I leave I'm no good to them. Out of sight. Out of mind.'

'Come on, Dad. You must have mates. You been there thirty-two years — twenty-eight years on salary. Wait and see.'

Dad worried, slept badly and had to see a doctor.

'It's stress and anxiety,' he was told. He got piles. The Church prayed. We waited for the right answer.

When Dad got a good pension and a very good lump sum, he regained his old confidence and thanked our Creator. Such a large sum of money had never come into the family and we talked of it with respect.

Dad had always hankered after going home and decided that's what he would do.

'I'll go in for a grocery shop. I'll go and see how the land lie.'

'Will you sell this house, Dad?'

'I think I'll rent it out and then sell it.'

So there the matter rested. Just before Christmas Dad stopped work. Ansel sent me a gift of a beautiful clutch bag with extravagant embroidery and sequins.

Darling love Marvella,

The girl of my dreams. This purse with the sequins and handwork, I hope, will show you what I sincerely think about you. I went into the shop and saw it. At once I said, 'Wrap it up. I want it for a very nice lady, my intended.' So let it please tell you that you are loved in a very firm and determined way. Last night I dreamt of you. I dreamt I was singing a song to you. I can't remember the words but it was beautiful. The congregation clapped me.

Sorry about your dad. There is scope for him over here. Tell him to come for a trip. I will be glad to put a little project of mine into his hands. I haven't started it yet though. Your mother wrote to me about the wedding. I agree with everything you arrange because my family would celebrate the Second Sunday after the wedding. You must know things will be difficult. Life is hard here, but together we will climb Mt. Roraima.

We'll all have a fine time.

My love to you, Ansel

My aunts were unhappy with the goings on at the Church. The young people were forgetting about its strict teachings, even the girls. My Auntie Mave caught out a few by asking for their help in a certain matter. Of the pill. Good Lord, fancy talking to sixteen year-olds about contraception! Anyway, she caught them out just as if she had thrown them a catch.

'Be careful,' she said. 'Although I never seen a baby-preventing pill, I am frightened of all of them, even Aspro. You all ever seen one?'

The girls nudged each other. Then Marsha, whose cunning ebbed and flowed like the tide, said, 'I can't talk about all the different kinds. But the doctor gave me one that suit me.'

My auntie's mouth fell open. She was so overcome she dropped her collection plate and didn't pick it up. She looked at poor Marsha with fire-eyes.

'You're no good, Marsha. Sin is eating you out.'

'I'm only on the pill. I don't do anything.'

'I don't believe it. You look like a girl who do things.'

'I don't. I am not sinful. I just take them pill.'

'Leave the girl alone, Aunt, or I'll go over and ask Mr. Davidson some questions.'

She took the hint but she was still convinced of the evil and disgrace to come. She wanted no part of it. She had been Anglican in the beginning. She would be Anglican in the end. She would leave the church before condoning sin.

Aunt Julie, too, was unhappy with the congregation, though for other reasons. They were slack. Full of slackness from head to foot. She did not want to be present when bad manners and slackness took over. 'No, man. Never. You know what I mean, Marvella. I rather be somewhere else.' She, too, would leave.

The whole of my family life, if I looked at it carefully, was a series of 'laugh-stories' They were all comedians, though serious and convinced comedians. Even Mum and Dad at times.

Dad had always put one foot in the church. He took what he needed and threw away the grounds and the stupidness. His fear of poverty, that had once drawn him to the church, had ebbed away. But it was the church that had helped his mother with her swarm of children. When all the bargaining with his employers was going on he said, 'Marvella, I fear poverty like it is a dreadful disease. I saw such poverty in my childhood. My own parents were so poor. My grandmother had twelve children and my mother was given away to strangers. She suffered till my dad married her. He taught me the fear of poverty. Before I become so poor like them —when I have to wear rags—I will lay down and die.' Now all that was behind him.

He stopped humming to ask, 'Have you gone right off my son, Ansel? He wrote me. Says you must write him, or his heart will spatter over his pillow.'

'So many things are in my head, Dad. I can't settle. My boss is off sick. There's so much to do at work. We're all busy but I'll write tonight.'

I was getting fed up with the distance. There was no direct dialling to Guyana then and calls were always difficult to make. Sometimes, the preparations for the wedding, took over my mind. Even 'became' Ansel, in a strange sort of way. I gathered my thoughts together, softened my thinking and wrote.

> My dear beloved Ansel,
> At this time I miss you more than words can ever tell. Dad said you want him to come over and supervise a project. He has ordered the things you want and they have been sent. He says it is a man-to-man job and he won't tell us but he is looking forward to the trip.

Something is weighing on my mind. Do you think we can push back our wedding to August? It's only two months and I will be able to ship over what I want. I know it might hurt your feelings but I have an urgent case here to deal with. My aunts want to go their own way. They have been with us since God knows how long. Ever since I can remember. Of course, Mum is upset. Encourage her to come over too. I can handle my aunts and the air will be cleaner when Mum returns. And now news about us — pleasant news. Easter is coming up. Dad's work uncertainty spoilt our Christmas but we are looking forward to Spring with nice flowers: tulips, daffodils and wallflowers. They are the nicest. My favourite with a most wonderful smell. *That* never changes. Year after year. The same colours and smell. Isn't that wonderful. Isn't God good?

I hope they are not overworking you and using up your good ideas. I don't want to make you fed up but I wish you were near to hug me, hold my hand and give me a specially nice kiss. I'll put a drop of my scent on this letter.

I love essence of wallflowers. My special scent. And it's for you, kind and gentle man.

Respect and love

Marvella, your true love

Mave had brought Marsha before the congregation. Sherri, who had returned a week before Easter, said we should attend.

Marsha, dressed in black, angry and dry-eyed, said she was on the pill because, 'People get attacked. Things happen to people.'

When my aunt saw us she whispered to the pastor to give Marsha a good talking to. But Marsha would not listen to him.

'I am a feminist,' she said. 'I don't know much about it yet but I am learning. I'm going to the meetings. No more of this sour-faced church for me. I heard you all say I tremble my backside when I walk. I done with church.'

To show everyone she meant it, she tore up her membership card and walked out. We followed her into McDonalds. We each bought root beer and sat talking about the narrow-minded elders.

My Auntie Mavis came in for a great deal of criticism and name-calling. Names like Witch, Sniffer and Ole Higue were hurled at her. I coughed disapprovingly.

'You know what I mean,' said Marsha. 'They like hungry people selling sweet food and not able to eat it. You know what I mean? The world, the flesh and the Devil lick they skirt like fire.'

Certainly I knew what she meant. They were two young-ish women, 54 and 56, who had been cast aside by life for years. From moment to moment, Mave did not know if there was space or sparks in her head. And as for Julie, she reminded me of Mrs. Gould, my Teacher in Infant School. She didn't like teaching us, so she talked to us in words that were not of our world. We thought her slightly touched when she yelled, 'Don't stand there wondering if it's fifteen or sixteen.'

Years later she told us it was a line out of *Winnie the Pooh*. Who was that for heaven's sake?'

My aunt's voice came back: '*Don't blaspheme, Marvella! You want make I wash you lip-top with soap?*' I heard her shout across the years. Then I heard myself again. '*No Aunt, pray for me I will never blaspheme again.*' '*Kneel down. Make we pray. Happy is the man who fears the Lord and finds great joy in his commandments. Praise the Lord. Blessed be his name. Ever more!*'

'Ever...'

'You said something,' asked Sherri. 'Marvella, you aren't turning into a head-case? Your thoughts gone to the moon?'

'No. No. Just thinking. You OK, Marsha? Don't let things trouble you; they will pass.'

We went home.

I had been so occupied with my thoughts, I hadn't drunk my root-beer. I was still desperately thirsty. Sherri made tea while Marsha and I talked.

'You know, we might have had 'affairs' if we had no Church to look up to,' Maria said.

'Go on.' I was interested in her reasoning.

'I mean... the congregation said sex is a no go area and we don't do sex.'

'I suppose you're right,' I said. 'But what of them, the congregation?'

'They want to save us from hurt. From pain. It's their way of helping us. Tight control. It's for our own good.'

'Then why the pill, Marsha?'

'Marriage or no, I don't want babies. Rob and I can marry any day but it will be years before I get babies. Mum had seven of us. Two in Jamaica. Two in care. Four brothers and sisters, I don't know. It's not right. It's like taking the pill for my Mum and me, and doing what Mum should have done.'

Sherri brought us steaming cups of tea. I watched as she stirred three heaped tablespoons of sugar into it. No wonder she was round, plump and bouncy.

That evening I discovered one other important thing. I had never *really* looked at anyone except Ansel. He had come in from outside, so my powers of observation had functioned. Ask me to describe my dad and I would have said he had a smiling round face and missed his particular features. Mum always said, 'Don't look, don't see. Don't see, don't know. Don't know, can't tell.'

The same thing went for my aunts. They were getting more serious, more corrective, their tongues ready to lash you down. But they did not see, did not truly take in the details of their world. They felt. We all felt. That's why the world hurt us so much. We were a feeling family, like thousands of others. I lay on my bed, my palms under my head, and stared at the ceiling. My eyes flitted from object to object. Living was a way of seeing. Oh, I saw dust on the objects in my room. Dust as unclean. I saw dust all right. I closed my eyes. I felt dust too. Feeling was seeing the links within the patterns of my world.

I must have dozed off. When I awoke it was seven. My mother was standing beside me. She had clear brown eyes, a well-cut nose, a frill of mouth. I took her hand. I noticed that she had long, thin exquisite fingers. I noticed...

'You're tired?'

'A bit.'

'I heard they warned Marsha. But she walked out.'

'Blame never did any good. They want her youth. They are jealous of it. I have a letter to write.'

'Dad has got his ticket to Guyana.'

'When is he going?'

'Monday — he got four days.'

'He has to get a visa for Guyana.'

'But he was born there.'

'It makes no difference.'

'I'd better tell him.'

'He will take my letter to Ansel?'

'There is one outside for you.'

Dad was going just in time for the Easter celebrations. He said, 'You know, I had forgotten about the kite-flying on Easter Monday. My grandfather used to tell me that it was to celebrate the resurrection. But my grandmother said, No, the Chinese started it when they came here. I didn't care, I flew a wicked kite with a razor blade on the tail to send other kites flying. That really impressed the girls.'

'Is that true, Mum? Were you impressed?'

Mum laughed.

'Did Dad look anything like Ansel, Mum,' I teased.

'The hat or the suit?' she said. We laughed again. I read his letter.

CHAPTER FIVE

My dear Marvella,

My love, my only love. I send you my greetings and hope that your happiness like mine knows no bounds. My little project is coming on nicely and will progress further when your dad comes to give me a hand. Well, my father went to Canada for a little holiday. He decided to marry Miss Milly and take up residence there. Miss Milly is as far from my mother as bread is from chocolate, but my father is a big man and knows his business. I wish him well. It's years since I saw Miss Milly, a 'mimmish' woman, always making people laugh. She is slight in size and one of her sons is working here as a veterinarian. I can't recall the face in detail. My friend Chandra Lal told me that according to the planets the seventh of August is a good date for our wedding. What do you think? It's a Saturday. So if you and your family agree you can print the invitation or send me the wording you want and I will print. Send me the number. How is everyone by your side? I hear your aunts don't like the movements of the young people at Church. Things change and I am sure strictness will chase them away from the gathering. I still remember the shops in England. Now stores are closing here and street sellers taking over. I still miss you. I always miss you and between the two points is my love for you. I look at your photo and give it a little kiss goodnight and wish you to do the same. I would rather it was you.

All and best love,
Ansel

'Sweet,' I thought. I was always fascinated by the way he made his points in a round-about folk-tale sort of way. Yet Dad's trip was the matter to be thought about. He visited the High Commission and had a long wait, though in the end everything was fine. However, they didn't say, 'Hey, you're native. Take this visa.' He had to pay for it because he has a British passport. Whilst his heart is with Guyana, he feels there's little choice about that. With a foreign passport, people coming into Britain have to line up under 'others' and answer questions. So for peace of mind, we give up a bit more of our identity. A hand cut off. A foot cut off and so on till we are so small, we count for nothing, with so many missing pieces.

We saw Dad off, bag and baggage. Mum was a little sombre, a little sad. Dad, laden with goods for Ansel and others, waved happily at us. We tingled to know what he was going to do in Guyana. I was sure Ansel had some kind of marketing scheme hatching in his head. We would hear in due course. Ansel's note from me read.

My sweet Love,

In a hurry. A few gifts for you. Sorry to hear of the hardships and high prices. Sorry too about the drop in the Guyana money. Keep heart till better times show.

All love, Marvella

The next day we knew that Dad would have arrived in Guyana, since no news of accidents or mishap had been broadcast. He would be at home enjoying the weather and visiting his friends and family. He had taken the wording of our invitations to give to Ansel for printing and distribution. The wedding party accompanying me would, I knew, be small, consisting of Mum, my godmother, my aunts, Sherri and me. My godfather lived in Guyana. He did not like living in Britain and had returned home in 1958, while my godmother continued here with Sherri.

With Mum, I settled down to sewing some cotton dresses for myself. It was like a sewing party most weekends when my friends came round to help. Marsha invited herself too and regaled us with the ABC of feminism as she had once done about religion.

'Women belong to themselves,' she said. 'They are not subject or object, cattle or things. They are free to say what they want, what they will or will not do. Assert themselves. If women need emotional support they get it from other women. Women should really, really assert themselves. Aggression is overreacting. Bad for the blood pressure.' On and on she went.

When she paused for breath, I said, 'But what does feminism do for black women like us?'

Nobody was prepared to tell me so we let the matter drop. I said that I liked being a woman and wanted to do traditional things which some girls were taught to expect and others to despise.

I tried on my dresses. They looked neat and fresh. I was happy. Both Dad and Ansel wrote. They were busy renovating a house where Ansel's father and his new wife would live. Just as I relaxed, Mum came in with a long face. She had been given notice of redundancy. A weekly wage earner, they would pay her a pittance in compensation.

'After all these years,' she huffed. 'After all these years.

Everywhere they cutting away. Taking jobs! It is the Prime Minister's fault. That woman. She don't care.'

'You don't need the money, Mum. We're OK. You and Dad never had time for each other. Now you do. Make the most of it. Enjoy this time. No more hustle. No more pressure. You'll be on a one-way street.'

Biting back her tears, her anger, Mum nodded. She then rushed out of my room, pretending that there was some dust in her eyes. I read Ansel's letter.

> My dear beloved Marvella,
>
> I am truly proud of you. Your dad told me of your brave defence of Marsha. You are fair-minded and that is a good thing. I received the list of names and the wording for the invitation. I will fill in my father's name after 'son of'. It should read 'son of Pastor Jackson Abraham McKay'. The whole thing makes me feel like somebody — just as if I am reading of someone else. I will stick to the hundred invitations on my side. My aunts, as I said, will arrange the Second Sunday celebration to keep everybody happy.
>
> Your dad threw himself into the project. He makes sure the work goes on when my back is turned. By the end of May everything will be shipshape. I'm just touching up things. My father is not coming back just yet. He is getting on with Miss Milly. He know if he do wrong she will whip him when he lay down to sleep.
>
> Your true love,
> Ansel
> PS: Thanks for the brief note — not my usual — and the shirts you sent. Always write a long letter. I get a transfusion when I read.

I sent him two letters, the one I had written after our engagement and this one.

My dearest, sweetest man,

The months are rushing by. I am so excited. I imagine my wedding and me in my milk-white dress. I hope I look nice for you. Mum has missed Dad so much she is coming over as soon as she gets her redundancy money. She took the redundancy hard at first, but later she accepted it as a good thing. They never had time to taste their life, which is like a good stew with many flavours. It was always hurry-hurry, anxious-anxious. They can really get to know one another, not as husband and wife — subject and object as Marsha would say, but as person to person. Mum has been very helpful. I know mothers are supposed to help but she has gone beyond that. Look after both of them while I am here with the aunts. I don't see much of Mr. Davidson but I believe Mr. Jones really has the hots for Aunt Julie. He looks at her with so much longing and touches her as if she's marked 'Handle with Care'.

They are always singing your praises, telling me how lucky I am. I know and I thank whatever God it is that made you write.

I hope you are keeping well and not over-working. How is marketing? I am so glad you respect and trust my dad. He always said God makes each day, but it's up to us to use it well.

All and best love,
Marvella

My aunts had more space to think of as their own after Mum left. They had never acted as if they felt they were intruders but they had no husbands and Mum did and that

70

fixed their position in the eyes of the church. In our church, emotional attachments between single older people weren't forbidden or frowned on, but they were just treated as if they were stuck in quicksand. Something about love filled us so full of guilt that we drowned in it. So when Mr. Jones boldly came out and proposed to my aunt in the presence of the pastor and the congregation, it was as if they felt they had to have the whole congregation's approval. The pastor, a chunky man with a lot of muscles under his skin, looked them over as one does a leg of mutton before purchase. He smiled, but his dimples stood still. Then he said, 'So be it.' That was all he said. 'So be it,' as if he had rapidly considered every aspect of intimacy between them before sanctioning it. He glanced at me and then placed his broad, lumpy torso between them and me, cutting off my line of vision.

My aunts felt that, out of respect, Dad and Mum had to be told before the marriage could take place at the Registry Office. I told them not to wait. I would explain to my parents. So they were married and Mave, Mr. Davidson and I accompanied them. Mave and I were the witnesses who signed the register.

Mave, although lonely and unhappy, was not grudgeful of her sister's luck. She would carve out something for herself at some future time. She helped her sister pack up and leave for Mr. Jones' house. He had never married, this small, slightly-built, mixed-race man. He was slow to decide, but when he did, he stuck to his guns. He had a wife now and behaved like a new man. They became a truly respectable couple and their past indiscretions were forgiven by the Church.

Mr. Davidson, though, continued in and out of the shadows with my Aunt Mave and she became so frustrated she rejoined her old Anglican Church and found other good causes. Once a week she helped at St. Martin's-in-the-Fields. I came slowly to realise she had an enormous need to mother cats, dogs, drunks, children, and devious, two-faced men like Mr. Davidson. She had her weaknesses, the normal ones like jealousy and anger, but I began to like her more.

That weekend Sherri turned up. She was enjoying her course, learning to make candles to bring light to African villages. She would, I was certain, be very resourceful in whatever wild bit of the world she found herself. After the wedding, Sherri would start her life as a missionary and teach in a country chosen for her. If she liked the work, she would dedicate her life to it.

That triggered off fresh doubts about *my* future. My marriage could fail. Marriage is a job of caring that goes on and on for years. Was I really committed enough to stay the course a whole lifetime?

'Dinner ready, Marvella,' Aunt Mave said, 'but I can hold it for a while. Letters come from your dad and from Ansel.'

In his letter Dad said how pleased he was about Aunt Julie's marriage. 'I always thought there was good in Mr. Jones. Draw out three hundred pounds from the family account and give it to your aunt. I should hate her not having a single pound to her name to pay for respect with.'

The following day, after work, I visited my aunt and told her of my dad's gift. She burst into tears, made as if to reject it, but suddenly snatched it and added it to the little bit she kept under the bed. I did not begrudge her. She had helped support our pastor for years out of her indifferent means, although he was a train driver and had a well-paid job.

And Ansel? What did he say this time?

My darling Marvella,
Last night I heard this record at my cousin:

Only you can make this change in me
For it's true you are my destiny
When you hold my hand
I understand the magic that you do
You're my dream come true
My one and only you.

It made my head spin. I only sing salvation
songs that praise God. This song was telling about
the wonders of love. They played it over and over so
I could catch the words. It is very nice. It is all I want
to say to you. Your mother is well. Your father too.
I love them a treat. Everybody loves them a treat.
They are two very good people.

All and best love,
Ansel

The telephone rang. It was my godmother, a woman who
spent a great deal of time observing and thinking. She and
Mum had been friends since childhood. She had always
supported my mother, giving her confidence. I hurried over to
see if everything was OK. Sherri was away and so I was
reassured to see her mother's fat, round face smiling up at me.

'I answer for you at your baptism,' she reminded me.
'And now I want to talk, to make sure that it's Ansel you love
and not marriage. I had him here in this house. I watch his
every movement. He is a clean, careful, self-respecting
young man. Caring and kind. There is one thing that I would
fault him on. He thinks women are helpless dolls. He will
want you to ask for his help. He understands his role as a
man in the ways he learn from home and school. Women
must be circumspect and not try to be men. He live for
respect. Do you love this man? Can you live without him?
I love my husband but we live in two countries. We still love
but I live without him!'

'Yes, Auntie Monica. I faced everything. Doubt, fear,

distrust, everything and I still like him. He is old-fashioned, I know, but I will have to lie down in my bed if I make it. I want to marry him.'

'Good, that's all. I think he would be good for you and you for him. You and your godmother must now thank the One who sees everything.' We sat in silence until she had said a short prayer. 'Everything, Dear Lord, is your grace. As it is, so it must be.' All my life, prayer was our appetizer, our seasoning, our sweetener.

That night, the moon was full. I was quite startled to see this golden globe of light in the sky and I felt glad to be alive in that minute, whatever the future held. The moon sailed above the trees turning the clear sky white gold and the shadows a darker gold.

A few days later Sherri came to see me. She had just returned from her training college. This time I felt there was something different about her, that this time what she had learned had been more deeply absorbed, become more part of her. They were teaching her to resist the urge to speak everything in her head.

'It's hard not to be able to say, 'There's a pretty bird'. You have to take these things into yourself, the sight and the object, as gifts from God. Then bless it and let it pass. You have to use words as a scarce currency, carefully, like water in the desert. You have to concentrate. It's hard, Marvella, very hard. But, hey, Marvella, do you know who I saw last week?'

'No, who?'

'Carlton Springle. He's been away in America!'

'Really. I never noticed.'

'He asked questions about you. Surprised that you're engaged. He said he's come back for you!'

'The idiot! Cheek! That pest.'

Sherri decided to stay the night and we continued to chat over our cups of chocolate. She confessed to feeling doubts about her ability to master so many different skills, all necessary for missionary work.

'It's not only God you have to talk about. You're out there in the wilds on your own.'

I yawned, and headed for my room.

I sat in bed and watched TV but I was really tired and soon fell asleep.

When I woke it had been snowing in flurries – late for the time of year – but it was not settling. I got up and made my breakfast. At around ten our door bell rang. My aunt hurried to the door. As I popped the last piece of toast into my mouth, she came into the kitchen carrying a most gorgeous bouquet of flowers.

My heart turned to syrup. 'Ansel. The love. Fancy him taking such trouble to show his love. Isn't that wonderful, Aunt Mave?'

She smiled but didn't say a word. Unusual for her. I read the card. My face fell. It wasn't from Ansel at all. Carlton Springle had sent it. The card read, 'I love you, girl, for what you are. I want to hold you tight. Right!'

I turned cold. I would return the flowers immediately. I called the florists as its telephone number was on the card. 'Come and take the flowers. The young lady does not want them,' I shouted.

'Well, Miss. That's not our business. We delivered what we were paid to deliver.' The phone clicked. I was in a quandary. He would certainly get the wrong message if I kept his flowers.

I asked Sherri to call and invite him over. An hour or so later, he came like a cock in the yard, smiling and familiar.

'I do not want these,' I said, pushing the whole lot upside down in the bin. 'I am engaged.'

'You can't be serious! I've heard about him. You going back to the dark ages — Neanderthal man. Engaged indeed!'

'You can think what you like. The dark ages is where you come from.'

'I like it when you're vexed.' And before I knew it he was kissing me. And I had let him. What was more he was patting my backside. And Sherri was there to see it all.

'Get off! Leave me alone!' I said. 'Get off!'

'You don't love him,' he sneered. 'I am the man for you. I will show that yard-boy how to love. I am the man to make you sing – the hallelujah chorus – in bed.'

What was I to do? I looked in Sherri's direction. 'You better go, Carlton,' she said in a weak voice. 'Nobody wants you here.'

He gave me a smug, daring, impertinent look.

'I am coming back. Thank you for breakfast. I am coming back for dinner.'

A way had to be found to stop this bold-faced young man from destroying my life. But words are words, actions are something else.

I lived in fear for the rest of the week. What if he'd written to tell Ansel of our meeting, and added a few details. What if Carlton returned? He was such a forceful man, dominant, able to use his maleness, as others would use a weapon, to defeat the enemy. Women were the enemy to be conquered and pelted with mud. God punish that man!

But I wanted to deal with the problem myself; I did not want anyone else concerning themselves with it. I would pray over it. As I did I realised I had been so busy I had been neglecting church. The following Sunday I attended the meeting. Carlton Springle turned, gazed at me, undressing me with his eyes. He came by me and whispered, 'What nice breasts and legs you have. God bless them and keep them warm for me.' Just then I got the spirit. I stood up and spoke of my engagement to Ansel and our forthcoming marriage. I asked for prayers to protect me from a young man who was attempting in every way to take advantage of me, bad-talk and low-rate my fiancee and thrust his unwanted attentions upon me. He had tried to lead me into sin by calling my breasts baskets of flowers.

'Would you name this man?' asked the Pastor. I looked at Carlton Springle's face. Terror in his eyes, pleading with me. Frightened of the shame of being named. The upright Youth Worker! I began to breathe hard. 'C... C... C...' I coughed, as Carlton Springle loosened his tie as he started to pour with sweat.

'Not this time, Pastor,' I replied. 'But if the young man even looks in the direction of my house I will name him. If he sends me flowers again, I will name him, and if he touches me with the tip of a finger I will name him. For the good Lord said, "Do not covet what is not thine own".'

'Amen,' came the voices.

'Amen,' said I.

'And Brother Springle, what do you say?' asked the Pastor, who knew his flock well. 'You speak for youth. What do you say?'

'Amen,' he squeaked.

I was rid of him, forever.

But for days, though, I could not find stillness in my heart. I could not discuss the matter with Sherri. I felt ashamed. What had I been doing, returning those false kisses? Why had I been so stirred, my emotions bubbling like rice in boiling water? It was a week before I was able to write to Ansel without feeling the need to confess. What indeed would I confess to? A moment of weakness. Half a moment. A few seconds. I wrote my true feelings.

My dear beloved Ansel,

It's nearly Whitsun now. As the days to our wedding grow less, my longing to be with you increases. Are you sure there are no girls there who love you and are trying to keep us apart? I am greatly troubled that you, Mum and Dad are over there and I'm here with Aunt Mave. Happily Sherri is here with me and my life is no longer like an empty tin.

Everything is as ready as I can be at this end. There is only the question of what to do with this house. Do we sell it or not? Mum and Dad are coming back soon I know. But when is that? A girl getting married should be carefree and happy but I am left here while my dad works on your project and Mum arranges my wedding. Temptation is everywhere.

Mave is going on a pilgrimage to Canterbury and is taking Mr. Davidson with her. 'If you loved me, you would be walking on your knees with me to Canterbury. You should be holding a big fat cross,' I heard her saying in her most commanding voice. Sherri will be here with me and my god-mother. My dresses look nice.

I'm curious about what exactly my dad is doing; it seems such a mystery. Mum wrote to say that the invitation looks really pretty in silver. The days are long for us. We have nearly three more months of 24 hours. Come what may, I will arrive a month before the wedding. I want to know all your old playmates and girlfriends.

By the way, someone sent me flowers. At first I thought it was you but in the end I found out that it was that fresh, young youth-leader in the Church. I could not be bothered to argue with him, I simply brought him before the assembly. He was shamed but not named. So there! I do so want you by my side. I must be patient, I know.

Lots of love. I give our matters over to God who keeps us all and points to the road we must follow.

Love,
Marvella

Four days later I received another bouquet of twelve red roses. The card read, 'From one who holds you very dear, across the seas, or very near. Loving letter to follow.' I was happy again.

I received this letter:

> Dear Marvella, my sad intended,
>
> I feel so angry about that foolish man who so disrespected you, but your mum and dad are soon coming back to protect you. Their work here is finished. It was not a big job, just a job that calls for eyes and men who don't take your money for nothing. My dad will come to see me and stay for my wedding. He will bring Miss Milly so you will meet up. You must not trouble yourself over girls with me. There isn't anyone else in the world for me, only you. You must believe that. I have never been a run-about, a sweet-man or a ladies' man. I went to England, fell in love and dream night and day of my one and only love.
>
> I hope you will like the place where we will live as husband and wife. I hope that you will find happiness and long life in it. Your letter made me think about you more. We should have got married straight away and I should have brought you back with me. Please don't break my heart, Marvella. I don't want anything to keep us apart, but things are coming together. Your mother is a wise woman. She is like a mother to me. A good, kind, useful mother. That man who sent you flowers, I will punch his nose if I ever meet him.
>
> Love from a distressed man,
> Ansel

I smiled. Surely Ansel wasn't jealous.

CHAPTER SIX

Confusion. Confusion.

From the cablegram Ansel sent me there was evidently a lot going on. But what? 'Mother and Father returning soon. Everything exhausted.' The message seemed heavily coded to me. Was Dad spending too much of his redundancy money? I didn't like it. Ansel had sold land. What were they really spending out on? Heavens, our people are such spendthrifts. Money bites into us like fleas and we must get rid of it. What were they really doing over there? I was the one who was meant to be getting married, and here I was, stuck at home, whilst everyone else seemed to be deciding my affairs. I was on the point of asking Sherri to find out from her mother if she knew what was keeping my mum there, but Sherri had lost interest in my affairs, or so it seemed to me.

My aunt Mave continued to play 'chase' with Mr. Davidson. I was at my wits' end advising her as to her romance. We had suddenly changed places, it seemed. For me, for the time being, love had dried up, had become a shrivelled flower dying of neglect.

When Mum and Dad arrived home, I was so full of pain and anger I could hardly greet them. We sat down talking around the whole subject of the wedding until Mum said, 'Put the girl out of her misery. Show her!' Dad placed a packet of photographs on the table. 'Go on, look!' he said. I opened the packet and saw pictures of a most wonderful white, two-storeyed house with a verandah going all round and rooms opening out onto it. There was a tree in the yard at the front of the house and seats like a necklace round the tree.

'Ansel was renovating this house for you,' Dad said. 'He is a wonderful young man. I am proud to know him. He is what my boss would call a man with principles.'

'The people respect him,' Mum added. 'It was a great struggle to do the house. He walked through fire to get the paint and nails.'

'And what about the girls? Tell me about them. You were there. You saw them.'

'I suppose some admire him. He can't help that. Besides he was showing everybody your photo.'

I smiled. 'That's good.' And the dying flower began once again to bloom and grow and send out a sweet scent.

'Are you going to sell up?' I asked Mum.

'Yes, we decided. Next week we are going to call in the estate agents. We have two months.'

'What you talking 'bout agents? Jenkins Tracey want the place. He offering me the price I want for it. I don't have mortgage to clear up,' Dad said. 'For years I bursting my guts working. Now I will take life easy. Things difficult there now, but Guyana could be a blessed place.'

'When last you heard from Winona?' asked Mum.

'A month or so. She still the same. Sometimes I think she mind mash up bad.'

'She back there with the boy she was with. Her intended. We have to wait to find out his real intentions. It look promising.'

'Ah-huh,' I said. 'Now only Mave left to get fixed up.'

'Julie and Mr. Jones gone to his island, Barbados. They'll reach home for the wedding day.'

Once more everything had fallen into place. I could see my parents before me. I would soon see all the other people I love: Winona, Julie and her husband and, with luck, Mave and hers. We were hoping that the family jigsaw would be tidy and respectable. Everybody with a man called husband.

The lights were on in my parent's bedroom, in the living room and in the kitchen, and already the smell of Mum's cooking, that particular rich smell, was invading the house.

I looked once more at the spanking residence waiting for me as a bride, at my silver-printed envelopes, my new cotton dresses, and the list of things I had sent — bedding, china and glass, kitchen utensils — plenty to begin with.

I could at last see the light at the end of the tunnel. Sherri and I went to the Tricycle Theatre to see *Goldibear and the Seven Duppies*. It was so funny, I really laughed. It was something Ansel with his childlike humour would have appreciated.

Mum had cooked chicken curry. The smell, like an exotic army, overran the house. A marvellous, marvellous smell it was. We set to eating with spoons. Not knives and forks. Dad always said a good curry needed fingers or spoons. Everybody wanted more, especially Sherri, who always talked of student food, hostel food and now missionary food.

The cat appeared. It had not been seen since Mum left last month, though I had been diligently searching for it.

'Hello, old girl,' Dad said. 'You look in good nick! You been staying with Midge Armstrong? She said she would look out for you.' Midge liked cats. She talked to them. I had hated going to her house. The cats rubbed themselves against my legs, but now I felt better about her. I had been worried that the cat might have been killed by a car but now here she was, safe, sound and fat. 'Midge, puss-puss,' I called. She looked at me and then went her independent way. A loner. A lover of freedom. Solitary like her kind. An only child.

'Did you want more children, Mum?' I said. 'It would have been nice to have had a brother or sister at this time — with all the work and all the celebrations to come.'

She gave me one of her cold looks and replied, 'You can want what you like! Is what God gives is the answer.'

We fell silent. Her with her thoughts. I with mine.

'God gives you children...'

'U'uum...' I interposed into the silence.·

After a while Mum found the words to reply. 'Yes, through your husband,' Mum continued.

I thought of Ansel and our children. Who would God make them like? Ansel with his long spider legs or me with my shorter, fattish ones? O for the wings of a dove, to go and see for myself his real life. Not yet my lover but perhaps someone else's, in spite of his piety and prayers. One of my workmates had given me a 'Partner Pillow', a long feather-light bolster that could be cuddled. Restless children loved them. I cuddled mine, pretending I was in bed with someone, happy in my fantasy. Ansel? Carlton Springle? His kiss commanding me to 'go to Barbados'. When we were children, Sherri and I 'went to Barbados' in our dreams and in our house-play and did all our forbidden dares there. Now I was on the way there with that man who had held me in a vice and kissed me. I was certainly going off my head.

'Marvella,' Mum said. 'You're a good girl. Straight forward. Free of twists and turns. Thank God for our church.'

I thought again about the precepts of our church, the church that each week met in a corner of a consecrated hall. It kept us on the straight, the narrow, the curveless road of life, with ideas half-expressed, words unsaid. Broken stones. Our dreams fade as soon as ever. Was Ansel alone in his room? It would be dawn there now. I could visualise him tiptoeing to the door, looking up and down the lane, letting her out and saying in his dark-brown staccato voice, 'Come back soon. Marvella in London sleeping, working, doing whatever. I am here with you.'

Fury made me blurt out, 'Dad!'

'What? What you so agitated about?'

'Is Ansel OK. I mean with girls.'

'There's only one girl he thinks about, or talks about — you.' Fury subsided. We drank coffee.

'A deceitful woman is a deceitful wife and the same goes for the man. Set your heart at ease,' Dad said reassuringly.

Marsha telephoned.

'Come over,' she said. 'Somebody lent me a film. I want you to see it. It's Woody Allen.'

'You know I don't like videos, Marsha. But I'll try.' As things happened, I couldn't go. Sherri and my godmother visited and for some reason the conversation turned to married love. I suppose it was for my benefit. I sat with ears pricked to hear what Mum and Auntie Monica, who knew such things, would tell those of us who didn't.

'You submit,' said Mum. 'What else can you do?'

'These are not Bible days,' Monica said. 'You have to play a part.'

'Like African singing,' said Sherri. 'Call and response.'

'Women must play a part!' I agreed with Auntie Monica.

'If you help discretely, you are judged wise. If not, you are judged too forward. The man is the teacher,' my mother insisted.

'I'm going out of here,' I said. 'I will find my own way with Ansel.'

'Women have rights,' Sherri said.

'That's politics,' returned her mother. 'Sex is one thing, politics another.'

For a few days I had intended to write to Ansel. I had put it off because I was fed up with all the talk of weddings and marriage around me. Big people thoughts which seemed pleated like a fan – convoluted is the word – but I don't like to use such words to talk with. But then I began to feel a bit guilty about all the agitation and suspicion I had felt. It wasn't Ansel's fault, but thought it best not to mention any of this in my letter.

Dear sweet Ansel,

My love. Now the days that separate us are getting fewer, I must concentrate on what is to be done.

I am all smiles when I think of our big day. My day and yours, when all doubts will disappear and we are one. I imagine our children. Some with your long legs and features, and some with mine. Mum says God gives children, but we are going to have them to celebrate our love.

All the preparations are ready, I hope. Mum says she arranged everything with Winona. I have known that family since ever and they are good, honest, clean people. Very stylish in arrangements — the father very upright. You must think if any creases are to be smoothed out. I am so happy that the long days and nights of waiting and dreaming will be over.

We have to leave this house as soon as possible, so in exactly four weeks and one day I will be with you. Imagine the confusion. The moving and the packing and friends coming in and out. I am becoming a woman, Ansel. All the pieces are coming together.

And the final piece will come when I am alone with you.

Best and all love,
Marvella

PS: How were the invitations received? Any talk against the London girl? Thanks for caring for Mum and Dad. Extra love for that.

I knew I had changed. Don't ask me how. I just knew that all my gently stirring, cooing, indifferent desires had begun to erupt. I was changing into a woman who wanted to be held, enclosed and pressed to a rapidly beating masculine heart. Mum and Dad were changing too, back into what they had been many years before, back into a comfortable cocoon of familiarity, half utterances and the will of God.

As for Mave, she had bursts of scurrying round after Mr. Davidson, chiding him and harrying him to stand still and listen, but her voice had become too familiar and he treated it as an unpleasant sound. Time ticked by. The Church sent an invitation to a Thanksgiving and Departure Party for us. We were delighted. My delight increased when Ansel wrote.

My own dear sweetness, (in anticipation)
Bad news. One of our windows was broken by a cricket ball. It looked like a sore in the glass. It's now put back. My one and only, sure we will have children, perhaps with luck and blessing after the first gun shot telling us to start. I am happy, turning into a soft man, laughing at everything. Only three weeks two days and five hours before I see your sweet face. Everyone is going to welcome you. The children will sing a song to you called 'Sweet Love's Serenade'. It was composed by Miss Matilda to the tune of 'God be with you' to celebrate your entrance into all our lives. Your mother and father are really good people. I miss them but soon we will all be present before the altar when I make you my own.

Sometimes shyness come over me for having to play a leading part but I've been reading about love a great deal and I'm sure the way will not be dark for me. Besides every darkness has its own light.

My sweet lady, I must bid you good night — incase you in my dreams and keep you wrapped up there till morning.

Kiss-kiss galore.

Your love, Ansel

We went to the church farewell party. A heartfelt affair. Prayers followed by songs by Miss Dorida Safeseige and recitations of two of Shakespeare's sonnets by her children. The deacons talked of our life in the church and greatly embellished the part we played. Mum and Dad sang, 'Goodbye people. Goodbye people. We're going to leave you now. Merrily we roll along. Merrily we roll along. Merrily we roll along over the deep blue sea.' Everybody clapped. I gave a donation of clothes, books and other things for a fund-raising sale.

We went home overcome with everyone's good will. In bed, I remembered Carlton Springle's eyes on me from across the room. I wondered what he was thinking. He had taken no part in the proceedings. The next day, I telephoned Sherri and she listened as I protested my hatred of him, especially since the kiss. 'Hungry and possessive it was — ahh — horrible. That kiss, uh!'

'You kissed him too. You didn't have to,' Sherri said.

'Did I kiss him? What could I do? A woman?'

'Bite him! But you didn't. You just let him kiss you.'

'It was only one kiss. One stupid kiss.'

'Was it? *My* arms weren't round his neck,' she said.

I sucked my teeth — something I hated to do and grunted, 'We'll change the subject. You're making things up.'

We talked about the shower-party my workmates had arranged. We were going to meet up in the local Wine Bar, so Maria could give me the cheque which was their contributions to my kitchenware.

'Will you come, Sherri?'

'Can't. It's youth-group tonight. I'm helping.'

I liked Sherri. She did not duplicate Auntie Monica as I did my mother. Sherri had her own view of life and had thrown out the folk-chinking and churchifying of her home. Her education meant something in all situations, while I used mine only to deal with matters outside our house — outside Mum and Dad. Did I use it with Ansel?

I was back home after two hours and very pleased with the generosity of my workmates.

'You're a lucky girl,' Mum said. 'Your dad and I weren't half as lucky.'

There was just one last party to attend. Marsha was holding a hen-dance send-off for me. Only close friends would be there – all women – and in privacy we could sing and dance and push against convention. Afterwards I knew the dance would not be referred to, as if it never happened.

When I arrived they were all there. My workmates and my school friends, all from our part of the world. They greeted me with a great deal of noise, imploring me first to please them, which I did with a box of chocolates, and later to dance for them. I refused emphatically. I asked someone to dance instead. They began to clap rhythmically until Marsha pulled me up to dance with her.

'Miss Marva is the bride to be
A husband man is kissing she.
Pam-palam, pam-palam
A big bad man is kissing she
Dance Marvella, dance, palam
Flounce Marvella, flounce, palam
Show us how the bed will dance, palam
Pam-palam, pam-palam. Wedding bed will dance.'

The clapping suddenly took me over. I began to dance, twisting, turning, bumping, boring, gyrating myself to breathlessness. Some instinct deeper than the sea and as high as the sky led me on. I danced, surprising myself, until I fell exhausted to the floor. I showed them that rice has motion when it's full of heat. They had nothing to fear. I was expressing my womanhood. I would know what to do to make good potato bake.

We talked of many things, saddened that my life here was closing down and another chapter opening somewhere else. I had been exposed to many experiences here — offered many opportunities — some of which I had taken for granted. But I had no deep feelings of regret, sorrow or sadness. I was going home.

I wrote to Ansel.

> My own sweet man,
> We are soon going to leave our house and spend a few days with Auntie Monica and then I will be on the plane. I will have three full weeks to find my bearings. I am sorry to leave my workmates but some of my life here is best forgotten. We had many parties but all is over now. Sherri, my golden godsister, is with me every step of the way, giving me courage when I feel that I will disappoint you in some way. I danced at the send-off with the girls and really enjoyed myself. Marsha and Claire showed me some good moves. It was good fun. I was good competition for any reggae-queen "Susie-May". (She is a 'wicked' dancer, as the young people say. Slack. Slack-slack.) But now I'm myself again. My decorum is still as it was.
>
> Mave has not gone to Sierra Leone with Mr. Davidson, but with luck they will meet up and come to the wedding. Dad gave them some fare money.

Two old people behaving like skittish children. All of us have our tickets.

When we were girls, Sherri, Winona and I used to go to 'Barbados' in our games. We did the things we couldn't do at home — like bathe in the rain, curse and play 'belly-woman', padding the front of ourselves with anything we could find. Why Barbados, I don't know. Do you miss me? Not long now. Excitement is rising like milk over a fire. Watch the pot, don't let it boil over. Wonderful times ahead for us. Life is nice, so very nice at the moment. I'm laughing here in my room all alone. And your sweet face is on every wall winking at me.

Have the cakes been iced yet? We are bringing a second set of ornamentation. I don't deserve all this. Hope my heart can bear it.

Love and plenty of it,
Marvella

I had given up my job and the days passed in contemplation. My life has been pretty uneventful, pretty sheltered, full of correctness and cleanliness and care. I never wanted for anything. Dad always gave me hugs; Mum mostly, when I was good or when I didn't shame her. If I didn't obey, everybody scolded me: Mum, Auntie Monica my godmother, my two aunts and Dad when pushed into it. Now I will be with Ansel. What will be his role in my life? We will be two people in one voice.

'I love you, dear Ansel,' I said. 'Please be good to me. Please let us be as my parents. Let us look forward to a long life in peace and friendship.'

I was ready to face the future. Sherri came in.

'Marvella,' she said. 'I met someone at the Centre. He says he loves me and wants to be with me. We are going to work in Angola together as missionaries and teachers.'

90

'When?' I asked amazed. 'Sudden isn't it?'

'Well, we don't control our ends. We go to the last phase of our training after your wedding. Then we'll get married. No fuss! God has shown us the way. He will lead us into love. We are two "likers" not lovers.'

I nodded. What could I say?

'I am still coming to Guyana. I'll be your maid of honour, but my wedding will happen, and then Mum and Dad will know. Can I rely on you?'

'Of course you can.'

We clung to each other and cried. What for we couldn't tell. 'It's not me crying,' I sobbed. 'It's my eyes.'

'You hear the news? Carlton Springle is going to be a baby-father, but the girl is a blank. Nobody knows is who!

'I knew it,' I said. 'I knew it! God help the girl. Thanks for telling me, Sherri. He was always devious, that devil-man!'

CHAPTER SEVEN

It was a long and tedious flight to Guyana, the land of my birth, the land where my children will be born to share history and tradition with our family, born and bred here in colonial times.

We began at last to descend in smooth drops of the plane until the filigree leaves of the dense forest below could clearly be seen. The plane touched down and after a while we moved toward the exit and slipped out into the water-clear sunlight.

The heat came like a knife-thrust as we crossed the tarmac. At the baggage collection point we found everything in a muddled heap and my heart sank. I thought it would take hours to collect my trappings and clear Customs, but I had listed all my purchases, so the duty was rapidly calculated and we were out surprisingly quickly. Dad, Mum, Sherri and Auntie Monica not far behind, were delighted to be home. They understood the voices and the nuances of this place.

My eyes searched the crowd. It was subdivided into family clusters, opportunists and strangers like myself. I bumped accidentally into the woman in front of me.

'Don't push,' she snapped. 'We all going. No need to bump and shove.' She swept her eyes like a torch over me.

Then muttered, 'Hot woman! You all hot over dere, hu-hu-hu. Push me if you got plenty money.'

I eased my way past her and stood face to chest with Ansel. We stared at each other unbelieving. Then we held each other close. He smelt of aftershave and guava jelly. I could hear his heart thumping against his chest. I hugged him again, unable even to say his name.

The next problem would have been transportation, but Ansel had organised all that and we were off to the village seven miles from the town. I knew all about it but Ansel was determined to tell me again the history of the village.

'You will like La Repentance, I think. I hope. It was owned by the French, the Dutch and the British. They all been here.'

I squeezed his hand. A lot depended on this. I eyed him in his white open-necked shirt, his jeans, his neatly combed hair. He had a new sense of himself and the old man in the grey trilby with the black band had vanished.

We drove through the once beautiful, now shabby city and then out along the coast road to La Repentance. We drew up to a large, squat building with a profusion of flowers growing close, or rambling over the walls. It looked like a page from an old-fashioned storybook. It was a beautiful house, happy with the spirits it had known.

Uncle Sonny, Sherri's dad, welcomed us. The house was neat and cool inside with jugs of jellied coconut-water on the table. They showed me to my room. Ansel helped me with storing my bags and, after promising to return and take me to view our own place, he left me. The house was cool with a strange, friendly, spicy smell.

How marvellous to be on mother earth after the confinement of the aeroplane. I stretched myself out on the sofa and put my thoughts at rest within my new surroundings. A kiskadee shrilled in the eaves. Dogs barked and children laughed. There was noise. Ebullience. Smells. A man sang in a strange language, (which Ansel later told me was Hindi) to the rhythm of a drum.

'You all right?' Mum asked. 'I want to hang up your things and lock the wardrobe.'

I let her in.

'Oh, Mum. I hope everything will work out.'

'Wait a little. See the house. Then you will know.'

She stroked my hair.

'You have brains. You will make things work. He has backbone. Land from his mother. Offer to visit his mother's grave. It would mean a lot.'

'Look!' I said. 'Blue chickens!'

'There are hawks about. Dyeing them fools the hawks!'

At around four, Ansel returned and we went to see our house. The houses in Guyana can be stylish and purpose-built. I did not know his finances, did not know what to expect. I had seen photos but they can deceive. This house was high with the 'bottom house', as it is called here, enclosed to form a large room with glass windows and window boxes. Upstairs were comfortable, spacious, well-proportioned rooms. Five opened onto a wide verandah, open on one side, enclosed on three. In the yard was a kennel.

'Why that?' I asked.

'You must have a dog here. To protect you.'

'It's London, all over again.' I laughed.

The packages were neatly stacked. After our wedding we would arrange our home.

'I had to buy some things second-hand,' Ansel began apologetically. 'Everything too scarce, too expensive here.'

I told him it didn't matter.

We started back for Aunt Monica's and walked out into the shadows, arm in arm. People sat on their doorsteps chatting. A voice from another direction started to sing. A strong, compelling voice, it drew my ears. The singer seemed to pour out something from his core, from both his brain and his heart:

'Shambolay man, love me, man,
Away Shambolay, let me sing doh ray!
Dark night teach me lover hey,
Shambolay lover man, maybe you play!
Oh Sham-am-bolay-aye
What do you want to do?
Take me, Sham-bolay — any —anyway
Walk me ah moonlight away from heh
Walk me at sand-beach
Till dew-day come. You hear!
Shambolay, sweet shambolay-a-ay.'

The palm fronds whispered to each other. The foliage tricked their shadows. The river flirted with the passing breezes and quite suddenly a night bird cried out my silent need to be loved, to be initiated there in the quiet darkness of the night.

'You know what I'm thinking?' I asked.

'I know.'

'And what I want.'

'I know.'

'Then why don't you.' A luminous insect swept across my face.

'I can wait.'

We kissed. My head was reeling, my heart agitated with desire.

'Hi Ansel,' a voice called. 'Dat you sweet-girl? Why you walking she so late? You no want we to see she?'

'I'll show you she tomorrow.'

We hurried home. Aunt Monica made us food. Ansel excused himself but then came back again. I saw him to the door. He kissed me softly and slipped a note into my hand.

Dear Marvella,

Love is like a mystery. I am glad of it. I am like a ship sailing to another world. All my love. My father will come tomorrow.

Ansel

The night noisily vanished and morning broke biscuit crisp. I couldn't wait to see my intended father-in-law. He turned out to be a serious man, aloof and correct. He spoke at length with Dad, as if that was the proper way to know me as his daughter-in-law. Then he came over to me, raised his hat and kissed me briefly on my cheek.

'This is my wife, Millicent. I hope you two get to like one another,' he said.

'Sure, honey. We will. She's a lovely girl for Ansel. Just right,' said Millie.

I smiled.

'Your father arranged the ceremony with the Reverend Sangster. Well God is God, and our Church has not yet been built. But soon. Soon!'

He was a tall man, in control of his body and his mind. He laid down firm lines of behaviour. Everyone showed him respect. The house was busy. Visitors everywhere! Suddenly Mave cried out. Everyone looked in her direction. Mr. Davidson had come. Relief all round. He looked crumpled and tired, as if he had walked the long way from London. Actually he had come by cargo boat from Trinidad, which he had reached by plane.

Next day Sherri, Winona and I visited the village market. Everybody was lively, full of laughter and yet full of guile. Some of the women were trim, strident and strong, toting loads like stevedores. Others were as marshmallows under their gaudy clothes. It was a friendly place. This was their life

— the place where they bargained, suckled their babies, gossiped and strove for a living.

'She is Ansel wife.'

'No, not yet. Next week. You can see she don't know nothing. She look real innocent.'

I smiled and waved to show manners and friendship.

'Show me your engagement ring,' said one. 'I never had time for that. He asked my father and then we married.'

Sherri was quiet, as if resolving something.

'Marriage is an act of faith. It's a chance you take,' she said.

When I returned home, Mum told me that some of Ansel's people were not pleased about something. I shrugged. 'I can't help if I don't know what's bugging them! Some people need poses and spite.'

But when Ansel came early that evening I did not mention this matter concerning his family.

'I want to take you to see a very old lady,' he said. 'We call her Mother Casey. She's very old and worthy of respect. These people in my village come from the same part of Africa and she knows the history. Black people from America always come to talk with her.'

I sucked my teeth.

'Don't be so touchous,' he countered. 'You can't come to La Repentance without meeting her.'

We visited Mother Casey, a tiny old woman with long gold earrings and two pieces of black wool woven into the grey hair over her ears. Age made her features appear etched, rather than moulded. I greeted her, bowing, shaking her hands and offering her sweets and stout, as I had been told to do. She seemed well pleased. She told me of the village, of Ansel's Amerindian mother and how the people had been brought to the plantation by a Frenchman called De Grasse before her mother's and grandmother's time.

'We worked the canes but we were Wolof people and we kept to our village. We used to grow peanuts here, but now we grow everything. And everybody is mixed up today. We no longer keep to ourselves. We even used to dress French but now that's gone. You go have long life with Ansel. You go have t'ree children — a boy, a girl, a girl. You will not have trouble — easy babies born. No other man will ever know you.'

I was greatly shaken. 'I didn't know I was going to a fortune teller,' I protested. Madam Rasia had made a blotch on my vision.

'She's not a fortune-teller,' Ansel replied. 'She only has the sight for some people.'

I was worried by the superstition but no one else seemed to think much of it.

'It's done,' said Dad. 'Forget about it.'

'I can't. That's why I feel like chipping up the dress and calling the whole thing off. That dress is sinful.'

'Chip up the dress?' Mum asked dismayed.

'Yes in truth.' I could hardly stop myself hitting something. Mum tore into the room to see what I had done.

Nothing! To do something like that would cause lots of pain to others, and I was, as always, a people-pleaser.

Someone must have gone to get Ansel to come and soothe down my ruffled feathers, because he returned at about ten looking really worried. He fell on his knees before me and implored me to marry him as we had planned.

'I don't like things mixed up in ways I can't accept. I don't want to have anything to do with superstition. I believe in God and I thought you did too. I can't understand why you took me to that old woman. Vanity, all is vanity.'

'Ma Casey is a famous psychic. She sees hundreds of rich, famous people. She won't harm you.'

I stood quite still, hearing my heart thump out, 'Shall I, shan't I?' a dozen times. It was shall. It came to rest on shall.

'OK', I said, 'but you know what I feel now.'

The next day I wrote to Ansel. Too many of his people were sulking. What did they want from me?

> Dear Ansel,
> Please bring your family to my godmother's tonight. I can't see each of them individually. So if you bring them all over they can see how fat I am, what style my hair is, if my legs are skinny and my teeth even. If they have any other questions, I can answer them. Sorry I have offended them. We are not used to telling the world what we are about. This place is not ecstasy-city, so I better get used to it. Love to you.
>
> Marvella

Around fifteen adults and four children turned up. In the village, children were everywhere at all hours. They sat around eyeing my every move. Mum, Dad, Sherri and my godmother officiated. To begin the evening, Mr. McKay said a brief prayer, my parents and Miss Milly named everybody, then we put on some local music: a record of work songs, que-que or pre-wedding songs, shango and shove-down dancing songs.

We didn't know whether they drank or not so we offered cokes, ginger beer and placed a bottle of rum in a strategic position. Soon tongues were loosened and the singing started. It led to dancing and when we closed down at eleven o'clock, all anger had been spent and a good time had by all.

I felt better too. I lay in bed mollified and able to recite my favourite bits from *Song of Songs* with great intensity.

'I am my beloved's. His longing is all for me.
Come, my beloved, let us go out into the fields
to be among the bushes.
Wear me as a seal upon your heart

As a seal upon your arm
For love is strong as death.
It blazes up like fire.
Fiercer than any flame,
Many waters cannot quench love.'

After that affirmation I was ready. Truly ready to marry.
I sighed and closed my eyes.

I asked Dad how the unpacking had been coming along
and how the rooms now looked.

'OK,' he said. 'Sherri knows you and she's getting things
the way you'd like them. Besides you can change it all later.'

Mave, Mr. Davidson and Julie and Mr. Jones appeared,
all in high spirits. Mr. Davidson talked of Africa, Sierra
Leone in particular, and about the industry of the women.
He had brought me pillow cases embroidered with sayings
like, *GOD NEVER LIES, BE HONEST WITH ME, MY
LOVE,* and *LOVE ENVIETH NOT.* He also gave me, last
of all, a hoop made from lianas from which feathers of
wonderful colours dangled. 'This is a dreamholder,' he said.
'It sieves dreams and lets the good ones come true.'

I was very grateful. I had never seen anything like them.
He told me they were made by the griots in Sierra Leone,
the storytellers and singers who kept time in their heads.

Mum and Godmother went through the arrangements
for the umpteenth time. Everything was in order. The time
for the rehearsal was fixed. Only two more days to go. We
hoped and prayed that it would not rain on my wedding day.

Each morning I looked eagerly at the skies, not knowing
what to expect. It drizzled a little on the day of the rehearsal.
That was the last time I was allowed to see Ansel before our
wedding.

Individual women visited me to give me advice or to tell
little jokes about their own marital adventures or just a
suggestive joke with a hidden meaning. On the night before

the wedding, women danced for the bride at the que-que dance — a kind of group dance with call and response melodies in the African tradition. The women had arranged it with Mum, as was the custom. Only women would be present because of the intimate nature of the songs. The bridegroom would be at his home entertaining his male friends, who would cook the food themselves. Women were forbidden to play any part in this ceremony.

The women came early to our house and demanded in song a drink from my mother. She gave them wine and off they went, an eager animated group to the part of the yard set aside for the dancing. When the spirit of the drink took them, they started to sing and dance.

'All you 'character' gone, gal
All you character gone.'
Dicky dum dicky dum, I want to dodo
All you character gone.

Then they changed to,

'Captain, Captain, put me asho'
I don't want to go anymo'.
Itanomi gonna frighten me,
Itanomi gon wuk me belly,
Itanomi gon drownded me.'

After variations on that theme, they changed to:

'De man come home
And he house bruk down
The grass fire burn around the town,
What kin' a fire mek all de trouble?
Mek de water boil and bubble?
De gal is de fire, de gal, de gal
De gal is de fire, de nice young gal.'

Mum and the aunts went out to join them and Sherri and I went to our beds under the mosquito nets, an oven with air spaces between. I tossed and turned, unable to sleep with excitement.

Soon I would be dressed in virginal white, walking up the aisle on my father's arm, pledging that all my life I would never grow different, never change, never view any other man. From now on Love would mean Ansel alone, for ever and ever. From this day forward the nature and the object of my love would be cast in stone. The deed was almost done. I ate a hearty breakfast in part celebration, part regret. Then I sat quietly facing the enormity of my hopes and my expectations of Ansel's companionship, commitment, unselfishness, generosity, care, concern, selflessness and priority. I dared not go on anticipating and then burying my hopes in this true and sincere man.

Why were there so many expectations built into names like man, woman, husband, wife, mother, daughter? Why couldn't we all be just people — adults with children's needs. Helpless, dependent, able to weep and worry, able to call out, shout if necessary, for what we need.

'Tomorrow. Tomorrow! For better but not for worse!' were the echoes in my head.

I promised myself that I would neither turn myself or Ansel into sterile deserts. I believe in the spirit of good, of choosing whatever is good in word or deed, that I would be so good a wife, so good a friend, that our children would, through the spirit, choose us to become their parents, and come to us through the love of two people who would always live in peace and grace and amity. A hard thing to do!

CHAPTER EIGHT

Open window. Dawn — a depthless grey. Imperceptibly breaking! Crowing cocks. Donkeys braying raucously. A smudge of yellow on the far-far horizon. A super dawn. Upright in bed, I await my wedding hour. I itch from the bush bath I was forced to take last night. Lemons and jasmine water. I am to become a wife today. The role I had been groomed for, born to play! The bright new wedding-band, the life to follow, Ansel's wife, all will be mine.

Time relentlessly went by. The space between Ansel's world and mine imperceptibly shrunk. I was certain I felt his breath upon my face.

Morning now, with an underskirt of pale light. Tall trees have impressed their shapes upon the new day. Dew lies on grass like shattered glass. A bird fluttered to the ground with a sweep of joy and then took off in its search for worms. Workers, like shadows in the mist, headed for the fields. Outside of the house, life had begun in earnest. Nature was all about. Hungry hawks determinedly watched for prey, while those chickens, dyed blue, sneaked cautiously, beak to tail, into a hole in the wall.

Daylight is now full and large, alive like molten silver in the shadows, like beaten gold where sunshine gathered. A yellow satin day, oy-yeh, containing the time when I would become woman and wife and mother in waiting. The day of initiation and awakening. The day of my ritualised surrender; the day of screwing up that last guilty memory of Carlton Springle and throwing it into the ditch of things forgotten.

I became conscious of the heat and then of my own thirst. I wanted to cleanse myself inwardly of dross and guilt. I headed for the kitchen and in my haste overturned some crockery. My godmother, fearing a thief, bounded into the kitchen to protect the sumptuous fare.

'What are you doing out of bed?' she asked sharply.

'Getting a drink.'

'Go back to bed. I'll get you one.'

'I'm not ill, not sick, not handicapped!'

'I know. You need sleep. You mustn't be tired today of all days.'

Like a child, I obeyed. Lay there thinking of what had gone before. Now the yard is fully alive with the voices of women. What do they think of our wedding? I had forgotten to ask my love the colour of his suit. Pin-striped trousers and tails? I wouldn't put that past him! The women talk. The wind is billowing with their voices.

'A good boy! A boy who knew God, who knew shame and did not flaunt himself before women! A good boy!'

'He does everything right! He got a London girl.'

'Dey talk like English woman.'

'But English people mostly white. Black people never English, na mine how long dey live dere.'

'Dey don't hold back. You see dem in the pictures?'

'Dey bold-face you know.'

'Hot-hot like pepper, especially when she don't able to rule.'

'But she's nice. A quiet girl. I see her.'

'I bet she got motion!'

It's all very amusing. I want to read but I am forbidden to

104

get up. I am locked in a land of shadows. I listen for rain, rat-grey, persistent. Silence! None today. I remember a poem of Tagore's about rain.

The palm trees in a row by the lake
are smiling, their heads against the dismal sky;
The crows with their draggled wings are silent
on the tamarind branches, and
the eastern bank of the river is haunted
by a deepening gloom.
Our cow is lowing loud, tied to the fence.
Men have crowded into the flooded field
to catch the fishes...'

'Marvella! Are you up?' It was Sherri's friendly voice.
'Yes.' I yell. 'Come in! Come in!'
'How do you feel?'
'Uncertain. Between the moon in the sky and the moon in the river. No one to share my reminiscences.'
'Yes! But how do you feel? Happy?'
'Once at a concert I had to recite a poem. I can't remember who wrote it. Miss David copied it out for me. It tells how people feel before change appears.

'Gather the stars if you wish it so.
Gather the songs and keep them.
Gather the faces of women
Gather for keeping years and years
And then —

Loosen your hands, let go. Say goodbye!
Let the stars and songs go,
Let the faces and the years go,
Loosen your hands and say goodbye!

'That's how I feel, compelled to say goodbye – to what, I don't yet know. There is a lot of overspill from my old life into this coming one, like plastic bags hidden in tall grass.'

Then Dad and Mum came in.

'Well,' Dad said, 'Today you begin a new life. Do well.' Mum said:

'Who can find a capable wife
Her husband's whole trust is in her.
She repays him with good, not evil
She is clothed in dignity and power.
She speaks well.
She is my daughter.'

She hugged me and we were joyful together.

Everyone helps me, loves me, gives to me. I am their child again. But it's not my birthday. Today will never, should never come again. Do brides, worldwide, share the same feelings of excitement and dread?

I ate breakfast. Lots of it. No recognisable taste! What in the world was it? Guava cheese sandwich? Cassareep on cassava bread?

'Be careful. Your dress won't fit,' said ridiculous Mave. No wonder Mr. Davidson gave her the runaround. I smile sweetly and travel from room to room viewing the dresses crafted with love and care. The mother of the bride. The aunts of the bride. The semi-sister of the bride and so on. Everything looked suitable, nothing over the top. The aunts won't upstage each other.

'Will there be enough transport?' I asked.

'Oh yes,' said Dad. 'Every single thing is in order. Don't trouble.'

'Dad,' I said. 'Squeeze my finger if I'm hurrying up the aisle.'

'If that's what you want, that's what I'll do.'

Outside the blue chickens are being fed. I feel a concerned tenderness for them.

At around ten, people brought presents but, out of superstition, were not allowed to see me. Time ticked relentlessly on. Three o'clock was not far off. Sherri and the bridesmaids would leave the house at a quarter to three, the others sooner. Ansel seemed to have dropped out of the picture. I was still wondering about his suit. I had imagined him in pin-striped trousers and tails. I asked Sherri.

'Wait and see,' she smiled. 'You'll love it! I nearly forgot. He asked me to give you this last night.'

'He did?'

'Seems to me, he feels a little inadequate. He wants so much to live a happy life with you.'

I read.

> My beloved and respected Love,
> In a few hours we will be, as they say, promising
> to live for better or worse with each other.
>
> May an angel of lilies and cinnamon guard you,
> With silver at your head
> and gold at your feet.
>
> That was what my mother would have wished
> for you today. I greet you with peace and offer you
> love.
>
> May you never weep
> May you always sleep
> Without pain but always with joy.
> And find comfort and protection
> Always beside you.
>
> Since I fell in love with you my heart has never
> been empty. I am ready to stand beside you and

promise to be your husband till death. Everything is ready. I am looking forward to leaving my old life in the corner. Throw it away without regret.

Love and respect,
Ansel

He is possessed by thoughts of me. What if I let him down? Last night I dreamt of a panorama of fire linked with beads of sparkling water. Today I read his words. I do not think anyone can be so wholehearted and sentimental. There is nothing extra-special about me. But only time will tell. I will grow in marriage and change. I will be treated differently by my family. I hope that he will like what the years make of me, and I am able to be comfortable with any change in him. I imagine Mum, her sisters, recall a photo of my gran. They kept their figures. Perhaps I will too. Men unreasonably ignore changes in themselves and notice wives who 'let themselves go'.

'Time!' said Sherri. 'The hairdresser is ready. Is here. Has arrived. Take your pick.'

She was indeed ready to start on me. Everyone was dressing amidst 'oohs and ahhs' of surprise and appreciation. Auntie Monica took charge of my clothes with Mum handing over the pieces to me. I was their child for the last time. My bath had been supervised, my hair, my underwear. All the rules were being observed. The hairdresser surveyed my headdress. She was amazed at the style – only to be expected from 'Brides of London'!

'Old, new, borrowed blue,' once again rehearsed.

And then the big moment, the creation of the big picture. The transformation. The bridal dress. Made to fit. Tremendous! Chic! I delicately slip it on, the bride disclosed.

'Gosh, you look nice. Gosh, my princess,' came the voices. I wince as I smile.

Sherri was in tears. 'You are so beautiful. Like a princess.'

Not again. Of course, I am the foam-fairy, shrouded in georgette and net! My earrings sparkle. My headdress is breathtaking. Mum and Auntie Monica turned me round about and having satisfied themselves that my dress and astonishing headdress – a burst of silver and satin in a sea of foam – were in order, they left for the Church. At precisely ten minutes to three, Dad knocked on the door. Sherri and the bridesmaids had gone, looking angelic in pale yellow with pink trim, and bouquets of pink flowers. There is a bouquet made of red roses and maidenhair fern for me.

It was my turn. Dad gave me my bouquet and took my arm.

'Lock up the house,' he said to the helpers. 'We want no mishap today.'

I stared into the mirror, forcing myself not to be cynical about the bridal uniform. It truly looked splendid. Worth the cost. If only Carlton Springle could see me now. A surge of confidence grabbed me. I envisaged a long and wonderful life flowing on and on into the years ahead of us.

'Come on, Dad! Don't forget to squeeze my finger if I'm going too fast. I'll feel through the gloves. They're lace.'

'A cablegram came this morning from Midge Armstrong. The cat's OK. It congratulates you and the family,' Dad informed.

My friends are loyal to the end! Effusive to the end! I am gloriously happy.

'Let us go, my baby, my angel,' Dad murmured.

People stood in rows and clusters outside the Church, which was full. We walked slowly up the aisle to a rather moaning-croaking harmonium, like a stricken soloist determined to sing its song. Murmurs of appreciation! I gathered a mass of faces. I began to look at everything, everyone individually. The faces, the flowers, the choristers, all the trimmings of Anglicanism. Where was the keep-this-simple Holy Spirit Church? We had adopted it as the children of necessity. We were immigrants no longer. Outsiders no longer. This was home, where my children would be born. Where we would, God willing, prosper and live in peace and amity.

The service! I wandered in and out of it, killing time until I made my vows in a timid voice. Ansel was more definite, more anticipatory. People smiled and sighed with appreciation. We exchanged rings, were told to kiss there in the presence of God and the people. It was then I noticed that Ansel, too, was wearing white. A smart white sharkskin suit! The man in white beside the woman in white wishing they would jazz up 'The Voice that Breathed o'er Eden' so we could flounce there at the altar. No wedding is authentic without that hymn. The synchrony of the voices hovered around me like bees about their queen.

Another hymn, and then the signing and the vicar's admonitions. The wedding was over. More music. The band waited outside the church to play us into the reception. We were spotted with rice and showered with rose leaves. People congratulated us, danced for us, wished us well. Our relations met us at the door, offered us our nuptial drink and then settled down for the toasts and the speeches, and of course 'congrats' from far and near. The formalities went on and on, the speeches becoming more verbose and ridiculous by the minute, while our guests wallowed in the ritual trimmings. The best man read the telegrams. My father-in-law spoke heartfelt words of hope to us. My dad praised my bearing and decorum which, according to him, had been inherited from his beloved wife, my mother. My godmother was more cautionary and down to earth. Then, as was expected, Uncle Buff, the village man-of-words, 'circa 1856', rose to address us. Before he opened his mouth people had collapsed. Dressed in his well-maintained wedding-three-piece, he began his learned few words to us, words that showed his erudition!

'Mr. Bride and Mrs. Groom, ladies and gentlemen of this social and auspicious assemblage, I offer my sincere congratulations not only to you all but also to this overflowing repast which reminds me of the Feast of Balthazar. Balthazar made a great feast for his friends and lords and neighbours and together they were such jubilous and bibulous people, they scoffed wine by the barrel in vessels which his old father, called Nebuchanezzar, had taken from the garden city of Jerusalem. That is what I am reminded of today. I will not take up any more of your precious and valuable time and ask you to please enjoy my melancholy and surreptitious rendering of 'Bless this House'.

The cheers were deafening although the man of words, as he was called, had sung it at every wedding for the past twenty years. Once more he had been seen and heard. Once more he had grasped his moment.

Ansel thought this was extremely funny. It was his turn to reply. He spoke without fuss, in a homely conversational tone. Then the dancing, led by Ansel and I, started. We cut the cake during a break in the dancing.

I was certain I missed a lot of what happened, but for me the best of the proceedings was greeting and getting to know the guests and the villagers. Growing-up in a different culture had changed me in many subtle ways. I laughed at different things, understood and used words differently, I had different values. Meeting the villagers was an enlarging of my world. I discovered, too, that my husband contained not only spice but ginger. He was witty too. And look what one could make with ginger: bread, cakes, biscuits, crystallised stems or brew it into beer!

I watched the young people enjoying themselves, eating, drinking and flirting in an open, honest way. Mr. Jones danced with his wife and Mr. Davidson with Mave. Sad to say, Miss Milly got drunk, and did a kind of dancing which was 'a notorious exhibition of commonness' according to Mave.

Her husband laughed it off and explained it with a wave of his handkerchief, like a piece of whitewashed cloud in the sunshine. Later, Ansel whispered, he was sure to pray diligently for faith and for his wife.

'It's not Milly behaving bad. It's drink. Rum and money is the root of all evil. Miss Milly has natural spells like migraine.'

Then suddenly, as the evening rapidly swallowed up the day, everyone seemed voyeuristically concerned about our need for sleep.

'When you ready, say.' Auntie Monica whispered.

'When you are ready to go home, tell me,' Mum whispered.

'It's OK. I'm having fun.'

Moments later Sherri was upon me like the Philistines of Mave's stories.

'You look tired. Go when you want. I'll come and help you undress.'

'Ansel can help me.'

'Not over here. That's my job tonight.'

'I'll give you a nod.'

Ansel and I went on dancing. He was teetotal, so there was no fear of spending my wedding night with a legless husband. We went on dancing. The music was so good! A string band from the neighbouring village had been playing pieces I had never heard. It had freely offered its services.

All of a sudden, Ansel said, 'I have had enough.'

'You want to go home? On our honeymoon? Where?'

'To our place — our own home. It's nearly nine.'

'No,' I said, 'it's seven. Well perhaps eight.'

I nodded to Sherri and we slipped away. We exchanged our observations about the wedding and were content that all had enjoyed the occasion. No honeymoon in distant parts for me. I had done my travelling and was happy to be in that little village by the sea.

I wondered in what condition I would find the house, but I need not have worried. Winona, Sherri and some of Ansel's cousins had made a most extravagant setting for us. There were flowers, a radio, a tape bidding us, 'Welcome to the Honeymoon Suite. We hope you and your lady will be comfortable'. It was from my workmates and arranged by Sherri.

We sat side by side, Sherri and I, and felt the warmth of an old and tried friendship. She helped me undress and change into an elaborate nightdress of soft, creamy satin. Then she disappeared into the night. I felt the slippery satin and thought of men in general. I was safe now. Safe. Forever.

Ansel entered. His legs seemed longer. Actually his whole body seemed to consist of legs.

'Hello, wife,' he said. 'Do you like my shorts?'

I read 'Love Happens' clearly printed on his backside.

'I have no choice. I have to. Love really happens.'

'How entrancing you are,' he began:

'My love — daughter of delights,
stately as a palm tree.
I will climb the palm tree,
and grasp its fronds.'

'I, too, know *Song of Songs*,' I said. 'Sherri and I used to read it nonstop for the rude bits.

'My beloved is mine
And I am his
While the night is cool.
Turn my beloved
And show yourself.'

I thought it would be always like this, down the years. Me undressed and prepared. The outline of our faiths identical. My prayers said, my wishes made. My teeth and hair brushed. A silly look on my face. He, after doing the same, would help me fold the bedspread and we would lie side by side. One part of the bed his territory. The other mine. I could hardly restrain my desire to laugh. But I managed to. I impressed a schoolgirl grin on my face. I listened.

The night was still as creek water. I could hear my heart beating, feel my pulse racing. We lay side by side, self-consciously inching towards our zenith, our heaven, a constellation of stars of hope about us.

'You're my life,' he whispered. 'My lifeline. Please, wife, do not change.'

I looked into his eyes, large and brown. They were full of happy laughter and tender anticipation. The moon stopped by our window, but only for a moment.

AFTERWORD

'The Man of Words' of the Guyanese villages of my youth, who spoke English in the manner of the Music Hall entertainers of the olden days, were magical creatures to me. The 'acclamatous' speeches they poured out at weddings at the drop of a hat, their 'verbulent' orations at funerals and the way they 'stretchified' the strings of Cupid's bow to send arrows to the 'disencumbered' target of a woman's heart never failed to thrill me. My aunt Ella, who was a brilliant teacher and a really good-natured woman, able to put every one at ease, received love letters which she read aloud to her sisters. I can still hear them laughing. This memory, with all its ambiguities and circumlocutions of the letters she read, has formed the basis for this story, celebrating the universal concerns of the young at a time when their feelings are like earthquakes in existence. With talking drums, lovers, if they wished, told all nature, as well as the people next door, of their love; but the talking drums, although they survived transportation to the Caribbean, dropped dead in the path of Christianity, at a time when to read and write was to be civilised.

In many villages there were 'officious' women and men who served as mouthpieces. They were fluent, insightful, deviationary and chock-a-block with subterfuges. They could somersault in debate and cross-question protagonists, black or white, with a comical efficiency. Their fluency and insight cleared the path for others and they performed with just the right amount of integrity in the name of truth, justice or love. As a child I sighed with envy at the joy and pleasure they aroused from any gathering with their self-invented English. I admired them greatly and celebrate their words in this book.

As for Marvella, the storyteller, I know dozens of young women like her – spiritual and self-respecting.

Beryl Gilroy

Also by Beryl Gilroy

Forthcoming in Spring 2001

Green Grass Tango

Alfred Grayson, a retired and widowed civil servant, decides to buy a dog to try 'not to be so lonely'. Sheba is his passport to the richly multi-racial community of dog-walkers and bench-sitters who meet in a down-at-heel London park. Here Grayson engages with cunning Finbar, theatrical Arabella and her absurd tango-dancing sidekick Harold Heyhoe, Jamaican Maryanne tortured by her demons, Rastafarian Rootsman, old Uncle Nat from Sierra Leone, tattoed Judy and abandoned Lucy.

Grayson, originally from Barbados, has passed for white and kept his origins quiet during his civil service career. But when he tries to befriend Maryanne and she remains suspicious, thinking him English and white, he begins to rethink his past.

In the park, characters, who would not otherwise meet, make unlikely alliances and feel able to expose various identities, or in Alfred's case begin to reconstruct one. Both park and characters have their times of shabbiness and moments of blooming glory.

This is comedy filled with a sense of human fragility and impermanence.

Price: £7.95
ISBN: 1 900715 47 3

Available now

Sunlight on Sweet Water

Beryl Gilroy transports the reader back to the Guyanese village of her childhood to meet such characters as Mr Dewsbury the Dog Doctor, Mama Darlin' the village midwife and Mr Cumberbatch the Chief Mourner.

It was a time when 'children did not have open access to the world of adults and childhood had not yet disappeared'. Perhaps for this reason, the men and women who pass through these stories have a mystery and singularity which are as unforgettable for the reader as they were for the child. Beryl Gilroy brings back to life a whole, rich Afro-Guyanese community, where there were old people who had been the children of slaves and where Africa was not forgotten. *Sunlight on Sweet Water* is fast becoming a Peepal Tree best-seller and is widely taught on women's and Caribbean literature courses.

Price: £6.95
ISBN: 0 948833 64 5

Inkle and Yarico

being the narrative of Thomas Inkle concerning his shipwreck and long sojourn among the Caribs and his marriage to Yarico, a Carib woman.

As a young man of twenty, Thomas Inkle sets out for Barbados to inspect the family sugar estates. On the way he is shipwrecked on a small West Indian island inhabited by Carib Indians. He alone escapes as his shipmates are slaughtered, and is rescued by Yarico, a Carib woman who takes him as, "an ideal, strange and obliging lover." So begins an erotic encounter which has a profound effect on both. Amongst the Caribs, Inkle is a mere child, whose survival depends entirely on Yarico's protection. But when he is rescued and taken with Yarico to the slave island of Barbados, she is entirely at his mercy.

Inkle and Yarico is loosely based on a "true" story which became a much repeated popular narrative in the 17th and 18th centuries. Beryl Gilroy reinterprets its mythic dimensions from both a woman's and a black perspective, but above all she engages the reader in the psychological truths of her characters' experiences.

As an old man, Inkle recalls the Carib's stories as being like 'fresh dreams, newly washed, newly woven and true to the daily lives of the community'. Inkle and Yarico has the same magic and pertinence.

This is a narrative of deep historical insight into the commodifying and abuse of humanity and an excellent book for close study in schools and colleges. Gilroy lays the past bare as a text for the present.

Price: £6.95
ISBN: 0 948833 98 X

In Praise of Love and Children

After false starts in teaching and social work, Melda Hayley finds her mission in fostering the damaged children of the first generation of black settlers in a deeply racist Britain.

But though Melda finds daily uplift in her work, her inner life starts to come apart. Her brother Arnie has married a white woman and his defection from the family and the distress Melda witnesses in the children she fosters causes her own buried wounds to weep.

Melda confronts the cruelties she has suffered as the "outside child" at the hands of her stepmother. But though the past drives Melda towards breakdown, she finds strengths there too, especially in the memories of the loving, supporting women of the yards. And there is Pa who, in his new material security in the USA, discovers a gentle caring side and teaches his family to sing in praise of love and children.

Price: £6.95
ISBN: 0 948833 89 0

About Peepal Tree Press

In the nineteenth century over two million Indians were lured away to work as indentured labourers on the sugar estates of the Caribbean, Mauritius, Fiji and other parts of the Empire. They brought the peepal tree with them and planted in these new environments, a sign of their commitment to their cultural roots.

Peepal Tree focuses on the Caribbean and its Diaspora, and also publishes writing from the South Asian Diaspora and Africa. Its books seek to express the popular resources of transplanted and transforming cultures.

Based in Leeds, Peepal Tree began humbly in a back bedroom in 1986, and has now published over 100 quality literary paperback titles, with fiction, poetry and literary, cultural and historical studies. We publish around 15 English language titles a year, with writers from Guyana, Jamaica, Trinidad, Nigeria, Bangladesh, Montserrat, St Lucia, America, Canada, the UK, Goa, India and Barbados.

Peepal Tree is committed to publishing writing which explores new areas of reality which is multi-ethnic and multicultural. We aim to publish writing of high literary merit which 'makes a difference', which challenges assumptions and leads to cross-cultural understanding. Our list contains work by established authors such as Kamau Brathwaite, Beryl Gilroy, Ismith Khan and David Dabydeen (and lots more!), but we are also strongly committed to publishing new writers.

Feel free to contact us for information about our books and writers and we'll do our best to help. We also offer a full mail order service to anywhere in the world.

Peepal Tree Press, 17, Kings Avenue, Leeds LS6 1QS, United Kingdom
tel +44 (0113) 2451703 e-mail <hannah@peepal.demon.co.uk>
website (from June 2001) http://www.peepaltree.com